GREAT TALES OF SUSPENSE

A WATERMILL CLASSIC

Cover illustration by Mia Tavonatti.

This special and unabridged Watermill Classic edition has been completely reset in a size and style designed for easy reading. Format, type, composition, and design of this book are the exclusive property of Watermill Press.

Printed in the United States of America.

10 9 8 7 6 5 4 3 2

Contents

H.G. Wells

The Magic Shop

I had seen the magic shop from afar several times; I had passed it once or twice, a shop window of alluring little objects, magic balls, magic hens, wonderful cones, ventriloquist dolls, the material of the basket trick, packs of cards that *looked* all right, and all that sort of thing, but never had I thought of going in until one day, almost without warning, Gip hauled me by my finger right up to the window, and so conducted himself that there was nothing for it but to take him in. I had not thought the place was there, to tell the truth—a modest-size frontage in Regent Street, between the picture shop and the place where the chicks run about just out of patent incubators—but there it was sure enough. I had fancied it was down nearer the Circus, or round the corner in Oxford Street, or even in Holborn; always over the way and a little inaccessible it had been, with something of the mirage in its position; but here it was not quite indisputably, and the fat end of Gip's pointing finger made a noise upon the glass.

"If I was rich," said Gip, dabbing a finger at the Disappearing Egg, "I'd buy myself that. And that"—which was The Crying Baby, Very Human—"and that," which was a mystery, and called, so a neat card asserted, "Buy One and Astonish Your Friends."

"Anything," said Gip, "will disappear under one of those cones. I have read about it in a book."

"And there, dadda, is the Vanishing Halfpenny—only they've put it this way up so's we can't see how it's done."

Gip, dear boy, inherits his mother's breeding, and he did not propose to enter the shop or worry in any way; only, you know, quite unconsciously he lugged my finger doorward, and he made his interest clear.

"That," he said, and pointed to the Magic Bottle.

"If you had that?" I said; at which promising inquiry he looked up with a sudden radiance.

"I could show it to Jessie," he said, thoughtful as ever of others.

"It's less than a hundred days to your birthday, Gibbles," I said, and laid my hand on the door handle.

Gip made no answer, but his grip tightened on my finger, and so we came into the shop.

It was no common shop this; it was a magic shop, and all the prancing precedence Gip would have taken in the matter of mere toys was wanting. He left the burden of the conversation to me.

It was a little, narrow shop, not very well lit, and the doorbell pinged again with a plaintive note as we closed it behind us. For a moment or so we were alone and could glance about us. There was a tiger in *papier-mâché* on the glass case that covered the low counter—a grave, kind-eyed tiger that waggled his head in a methodical manner; there were several crystal spheres, a china hand holding magic cards, a stock of magic fishbowls in various sizes, and an immodest magic hat that shamelessly displayed its springs. On the floor were magic mirrors; one to draw you out long and thin, one to swell your head and vanish your legs, and one to make you short and fat like a draught; and while we were laughing at these the shopman, as I suppose, came in.

At any rate, there he was behind the counter—a curious, sallow, dark man, with one ear larger than the other and a chin like the toe cap of a boot.

"What can we have the pleasure?" he said, spreading his long, magic fingers on the glass case; and so with a start we were aware of him.

"I want," I said, "to buy my little boy a few simple tricks."

"Legerdemain?" he asked. "Mechanical? Domestic?"

"Anything amusing," said I.

"Um!" said the shopman, and scratched his head for a moment as if thinking. Then, quite distinctly, he drew from his head a glass ball. "Something in this way?" he said, and held it out.

The action was unexpected. I had seen the trick done at entertainments endless times before—it's part of the common stock of conjurers—but I had not expected it here. "That's good," I said, with a laugh.

"Isn't it?" said the shopman.

Gip stretched out his disengaged hand to take this object and found merely a blank palm.

"It's in your pocket," said the shopman, and there it was!

"How much will that be?" I asked.

"We make no charge for glass balls," said the shopman politely. "We get them"—he picked one out of his elbow as he spoke—"free." He produced another from the back of his neck, and laid it beside its predecessor on the counter. Gip regarded his glass ball sagely, then directed a look of inquiry at the two on the counter, and finally brought his round-eyed scrutiny to the shopman, who smiled. "You may have those too," said the shopman, "and, if you *don't* mind, one from my mouth. *So!*"

Gip counseled me mutely for a moment, and then in a profound silence put away the four balls, resumed my reassuring finger, and nerved himself for the next event.

"We get all our smaller tricks in that way," the shopman remarked.

I laughed in the manner of one who subscribes to a jest. "Instead of going to the wholesale shop," I said. "Of course, it's cheaper."

"In a way," the shopman said. "Though we pay in the end. But not so heavily—as people suppose . . . . Our larger tricks, and our daily provisions and all the other things we want, we get out of that hat . . . . And you know, sir, if you'll excuse my saying it, there *isn't* a wholesale shop not for Genuine Magic goods, sir. I don't know if you noticed our inscription—the Genuine Magic shop." He drew a business card from his cheek and handed it to me. "Genuine," he said, with his finger on the word, and added, "There is absolutely no deception, sir."

He seemed to be carrying out the joke pretty thoroughly, I thought.

He turned to Gip with a smile of remarkable affability. "You, you know, are the Right Sort of Boy."

I was surprised at his knowing that, because, in the interests of discipline, we keep it rather a secret at home; but Gip received it in unflinching silence, keeping a steadfast eye on him.

"It's only the Right Sort of Boy gets through that doorway."

And, as if by way of illustration, there came a rattling at the door, and a squeaking little voice could be faintly heard. "Nyar! I *warn* 'a go in there, dadda, I WARN 'a go in there. Ny-a-a-ah!" and then the accents of a downtrodden parent, urging consolations and propitiations. "It's locked, Edward," he said.

"But it isn't," said I.

"It is, sir," said the shopman, "always—for that sort of child," and as he spoke we had a glimpse of the other youngster, a little, white face, pallid from sweet-eating and oversapid food, and distorted by evil passions, a ruthless little egotist, pawing at the enchanted pane. "It's no good, sir," said the shopman, as I moved, with my natural helpfulness, doorward, and presently the spoiled child was carried off howling.

"How do you manage that?" I said, breathing a little more freely.

"Magic!" said the shopman, with a careless wave of the hand, and behold! Sparks of colored fire flew out of his fingers and vanished into the shadows of the shop.

"You were saying," he said, addressing himself to Gip, "before you came in that you would like one of our 'Buy One and Astonish your Friends' boxes?"

Gip, after a gallant effort said, "Yes."

"It's in your pocket."

And leaning over the counter—he really had an extraordinarily long body—this amazing person produced the article in the customary conjurer's manner. "Paper," he said, and took a sheet out of the empty hat with the springs; "string," and behold his mouth was a string box, from which he drew an unending thread, which when he had tied his parcel he bit off—and, it seemed to me, swallowed the ball of string. And then he lit a candle at the nose of one of the ventriloquist's dummies, stuck one of his fingers (which had become sealing-wax red), into the flame, and so sealed the parcel. "Then there was the Disappearing Egg," he remarked, and produced one from within my coat-breast and packed it, and also The Crying Baby, Very Human. I handed each parcel to Gip as it was ready, and he clasped them to his chest.

He said very little, but his eyes were eloquent; the clutch of his arms was eloquent. He was the playground of unspeakable emotions. These, you know, were *real* Magics.

Then, with a start, I discovered something moving about in my hat—something soft and jumpy. I whipped it off, and a ruffled pigeon—no doubt a confederate—dropped out and ran on the counter, and went, I fancy, into a cardboard box behind the *papier-mâché* tiger.

"Tut, tut!" said the shopman, dexterously relieving me of my headdress; "careless bird, and—as I live—nesting!"

He shook my hat, and shook out into his extended hand two or three eggs, a large marble, a watch, about half-a-dozen of the inevitable glass balls, and then crumpled, crinkled paper, more and more and more, talking all the time of the way in which people neglect to brush their hats *inside* as well as out, politely, of course, but with a certain personal application. "All sorts of things accumulate, sir . . . . Not *you*, of course, in particular . . . . Nearly every customer . . . . Astonishing what they carry about with them . . . . " The crumpled paper rose and billowed on the counter more and more and more, until he was nearly hidden from us, until he was altogether hidden, and still his voice went on and on. "We none of us know what the fair semblance of a human being may conceal, sir. Are we all then no better than brushed exteriors, whited sepulchres—"

His voice stopped—exactly like when you hit a neighbor's gramophone with a well-aimed brick, the same instant silence, and the rustle of the paper stopped, and everything was still . . . .

"Have you done with my hat?" I said, after an interval.

There was no answer.

I stared at Gip, and Gip stared at me, and there were our distortions in the magic mirrors, looking very rum, and grave, and quiet . . . .

"I think we'll go now," I said. "Will you tell me how much all this comes to? . . .

"I say," I said, on a rather louder note, "I want the bill; and my hat, please."

It might have been a sniff from behind the paper pile . . . .

"Let's look behind the counter, Gip," I said. "He's making fun of us."

I led Gip round the head-wagging tiger, and what to you think there was behind the counter? No one at all! Only my hat on the floor, and a common conjurer's lop-earred white rabbit lost in meditation, and looked as stupid and crumpled as only a conjurer's rabbit can do. I resumed my hat, and the rabbit lolloped a lollop or so out of my way.

"Dadda!" said Gip, in a guilty whisper.

"What is it, Gip?" said I.

"I *do* like this shop, dadda."

"So should I," I said to myself, "if the counter wouldn't suddenly extend itself to shut one off from the door." But I didn't call Gip's attention to that. "Pussy!" he said, with a hand out to the rabbit as it came lolloping past us; "Pussy, do Gip a magic!" and his eyes followed it as it squeezed through the door I had certainly not remarked a moment before. Then this door opened wider, and the man with one ear larger than the other appeared again. He was smiling still, but his eye met mine with something between amusement and defiance. "You'd like to see our showroom, sir," he said, with an innocent sauvity. Gip tugged my finger forward. I glanced at the counter and met the shopman's eye again. I was beginning to think the magic just a little too genuine. "We haven't *very* much time," I said. But somehow we were inside the showroom before I could finish that.

"All goods of the same quality," said the shopman, rubbing his flexible hands together, "and that is the Best. Nothing in the place that isn't genuine Magic, and warranted thoroughly rum. Excuse me, sir!"

I felt him pull at something that clung to my coat sleeve, and then I saw he held a little, wriggling red demon by the tail—the little creature bit and fought and tried to get at his hand—and in a moment he tossed it carelessly behind a counter. No doubt the thing was only an image of twisted india rubber, but for the moment—! And his gesture was exactly that of a man who handles some petty biting bit of vermin. I glanced at Gip, but Gip was looking at a magic rocking horse. I was glad he hadn't seen the thing. "I say," I said in an undertone, and indicating Gip and the red demon with my eyes, "you haven't many things like *that* about, have you?"

"None of ours! Probably brought it with you," said the shopman—also in an undertone, and with a more dazzling smile than ever. "Astonishing what people *will* carry about with them unawares!" And then to Gip, "Do you see anything you fancy here?"

There were many things that Gip fancied there.

He turned to this astonishing tradesman with mingled confidence and respect. "Is that a Magic Sword?" he said.

"A Magic Toy Sword. It neither bends, breaks, nor cuts the fingers. It renders the bearer invincible in battle against anyone under eighteen. Half-a-crown to seven and sixpence, according to size.

These panoplies on cards are for juvenile knights-errant and very useful—shield of safety, sandals of swiftness, helmet of invisibility.''

'Oh, daddy!'' gasped Gip.

I tried to find out what they cost, but the shopman did not heed me. He had got Gip now; he had got him away from my finger; he had embarked upon the exposition of all his confounded stock, and nothing was going to stop him. Presently I saw with a qualm of distrust and something very like jealousy that Gip had hold of this person's finger as usually he has hold of mine. No doubt the fellow was interesting, I thought, and had an interestingly faked lot of stuff, really *good* faked stuff, still—

I wandered after them, saying very little, but keeping an eye on this prestidigital fellow. After all, Gip was enjoying it. And no doubt when the time came to go we should be able to go quite easily.

It was a long, rambling place, that showroom, a gallery broken up by stands and stalls and pillars, with archways leading off to other departments, in which the queerest-looking assistants loafed and stared at one, and with perplexing mirrors and curtains. So perplexing, indeed, were these that I was presently unable to make out the door by which we had come.

The shopman showed Gip magic trains that ran without steam or clockwork, just as you set the signals, and then some very, very valuable boxes of soldiers that all came alive directly you took off the lid and said—. I myself haven't a very quick ear and it was a tongue-twisting sound, but Gip—he has his mother's ear—got it in no time. "Bravo!" said the shopman, putting the men back into the box unceremoniously and handing it to Gip. "Now," said the shopman, and in a moment Gip had made them all alive again.

"You'll take that box?" asked the shopman.

"We'll take that box," said I, "unless you charge its full value. In which case it would need a Trust Magnate—"

"Dear heart! *No*!" and the shopman swept the little men back again, shut the lid, waved the box in the air, and there it was, in brown paper, tied up and—*with Gip's full name and address on the paper!*

The shopman laughed at my amazement.

"This is the genuine magic," he said. "The real thing."

"It's a little too genuine for my taste," I said again.

After that he fell to showing Gip tricks, odd tricks, and still odder the way they were done. He explained them, he turned them inside out, and there was the dear little chap nodding his busy bit of a head in the sagest manner.

I did not attend as well as I might. "Hey, presto!" said the Magic Shopman, and then would come the clear, small "Hey, presto!" of the boy. But I was distracted by other things. It was being borne in upon me just how tremendously rum this place was; it was, so to speak, inundated by a sense of rumness. There was something a little rum about the fixtures even, about the ceiling, about the floor, about the casually distributed chairs. I had a queer feeling that whenever I wasn't looking at them straight they went askew, and moved about, and played a noiseless puss-in-the-corner behind my back. And the cornice had a serpentine design with masks—masks altogether too expressive for proper plaster.

Then abruptly my attention was caught by one of the odd-looking assistants. He was some way off and evidently unaware of my presence—I saw a sort of three-quarter length of him over a pile of toys and through an arch—and, you know, he was leaning against a pillar in an idle sort of way doing the most horrid things with his features! The particular horrid thing he did was with his nose. He did it just as though he was idle and wanted to amuse himself. First of all it was a short, blobby nose, and then suddenly he shot it out like a telescope, and then out it flew and became thinner and thinner until it was like a long, red, flexible whip. Like a thing in a nightmare it was! He flourished it about and flung it forth as a flyfisher flings his line.

My instant thought was that Gip mustn't see him. I turned about, and there was Gip quite preoccupied with the shopman, and thinking no evil. They were whispering together and looking at me. Gip was standing on a little stool, and the shopman was holding a sort of big drum in his hand.

"Hide and seek, dadda!" cried Gip. "You're He!"

And before I could do anything to prevent it, the shopman had clapped the big drum over him.

I saw what was up directly. "Take that off," I cried, "this instant! You'll frighten the boy. Take it off!"

The shopman with the unequal ears did so without a word, and held the big cylinder towards me to show its emptiness. And the little stool was vacant! In that instant my boy had utterly disappeared? . . .

You know, perhaps, that sinister something that comes like a hand out of the unseen and grips your heart about. You know it takes your common self away and leaves you tense and deliberate, neither slow nor hasty, neither angry nor afraid. So it was with me.

I came up to this grinning shopman and kicked his stool aside.

"Stop this folly!" I said. "Where is my boy?"

"You see," he said, still displaying the drum's interior, "there is no deception—"

I put out my hand to grip him, and he eluded me by a dexterous movement. I snatched again, and he turned from me and pushed open a door to escape. "Stop!" I said, and he laughed, receding. I leaped after him—into utter darkness.

Thud!

"Lor' bless my 'eart! I didn't see you coming, sir!"

I was in Regent Street, and I had collided with a decent-looking working man; and a yard away, perhaps, and looking a little perplexed with himself, was Gip. There was some sort of apology, and then Gip had turned and come to me with a bright little smile, as though for a moment he had missed me.

And he was carrying four parcels in his arm!

He secured immediate possession of my finger.

For the second I was rather at a loss. I stared round to see the door of the magic shop, and, behold, it was not there! There was no door, no shop, nothing, only the common pilaster between the shop where they sell pictures and the window with the chicks! . . .

I did the only thing possible in that mental

tumult; I walked to the curbstone and held up my umbrella for a cab.

"'Ansoms," said Gip, in a note of culminating exultation.

I helped him in, recalled my address with an effort, and got in also. Something unusual proclaimed itself in my tailcoat pocket, and I felt and discovered a glass ball. With a petulant expression I flung it into the street.

Gip said nothing.

For a space neither of us spoke.

"Dadda!" said Gip, at last, "that *was* a proper shop!"

I came round with that to the problem of just how the whole thing had seemed to him. He looked completely undamaged—so far, good; he was neither scared nor unhinged, he was simply tremendously satisfied with the afternoon's entertainment, and there in his arms were the four parcels.

Confound it! What could be in them?

"Um!" I said. "Little boys can't go to shops like that every day."

He received this with his usual stoicism, and for a moment I was sorry I was his father and not his mother, and so couldn't suddenly there, *coram publico,* in our hansom, kiss him. After all, I thought, the thing wasn't so very bad.

But it was only when we opened the parcels that I really began to be reassured. Three of them contained boxes of soldiers, quite ordinary lead soldiers, but of so good a quality as to make Gip altogether forget that originally these parcels had been Magic Tricks of the only genuine sort, and the fourth contained a kitten, a little living white kitten, in excellent health and appetite and temper.

I saw this unpacking with a sort of provisional relief. I hung about in the nursery for quite an unconscionable time . . . .

That happened six months ago. And now I am beginning to believe it is all right. The kitten had only the magic natural to all kittens, and the soldiers seem as steady a company as any colonel could desire. And Gip—?

The intelligent parent will understand that I have to go cautiously with Gip. But I went so far as this one day. I said, "How would you like your soldiers to come alive, Gip, and march about by themselves?"

"Mine do," said Gip. "I just have to say a word I know before I open the lid."

"Then they march about alone?"

"Oh, *quite*, dadda. I shouldn't like them if they didn't do that."

I displayed no unbecoming surprise, and since then I have taken occasion to drop in upon him once or twice, unannounced, when the soldiers were about, but so far I have never discovered them performing in anything like a magical manner . . . .

It's so difficult to tell.

There's also a question of finance. I have an incurable habit of paying bills. I have been up and down Regent Street several times, looking for that shop. I am inclined to think, indeed, that in that matter honor is satisfied, and that, since Gip's name and address are known to them, I may very well leave it to these people, whoever they may be, to send in their bill in their own time.

Charles Dickens

The Ghost Chamber

The house was a genuine old house of a very quaint description, teeming with old carvings, and beams, and panels, and having an excellent old staircase, with a gallery or upper staircase, cut off from it by a curious fencework of old oak, or of the old Honduras Mahogany wood. It was, and is, and will be, for many a long year to come, a remarkably picturesque house; and a certain grave mystery lurking in the depth of the old mahogany panels, as if they were so many deep pools of dark water—such, indeed, as they had been much among when they were trees—gave it a very mysterious character after nightfall.

When Mr. Goodchild and Mr. Idle had first alighted at the door, and stepped into the somber handsome old hall, they had been received by half-a-dozen noiseless old men in black, all dressed exactly alike, who glided up the stairs with the obliging landlord and waiter—but without appearing to get into their way, or to mind whether they did or no—and who had filed off to the right and left on the old staircase, as the guests entered their sitting room. It was then broad, bright day. But, Mr. Goodchild had said, when their door was shut, "Who on earth are those old men?" And afterwards, both on going out and coming in, he had noticed that there were no old men to be seen.

Neither, had the old men, or any one of the old men, reappeared since. The two friends had passed a night in the house, but had seen nothing more of the old men. Mr. Goodchild, in rambling about it, had looked along passages, and glanced in at doorways, but had encountered no old men; neither did it appear that any old men were, by any member of the establishment, missed or expected.

Another odd circumstance impressed itself on their attention. It was, that the door of their sitting room was never left untouched for a quarter of an hour. It was opened with hesitation, opened with confidence, opened a little way, opened a good way, always clapped to again without a word of explanation. They were reading, they were writing, they were eating, they were drinking, they were talking, they were dozing; the door was always opened at an unexpected moment, and they looked towards it, and it was clapped to again, and nobody was to be seen. When this had happened fifty times or so, Mr. Goodchild had said to his companion, jestingly: "I begin to think, Tom, there was something wrong with those six old men."

Night had come again, and they had been writing for two or three hours: writing, in short, a portion of the lazy notes from which these lazy sheets were taken. They had left off writing, and glasses were on the table between them. The house was closed and quiet. Around the head of Thomas Idle, as he lay upon his sofa, hovered light wreaths of fragrant smoke. The temples of Francis Goodchild, as he leaned back in his chair, with his two hands clasped behind his head, and his legs crossed, were similarly decorated.

They had been discussing several idle subjects of speculation, not omitting the strange old men, and were still so occupied, when Mr. Goodchild abruptly changed his attitude to wind up his watch. They were just becoming drowsy enough to be stopped in their talk by any such slight check. Thomas Idle, who was speaking at the moment, paused and said, "How goes it?"

"One," said Goodchild.

As if he had ordered one old man, and the order were promptly executed (truly, all orders were so, in that excellent hotel), the door opened, and one old man stood there.

He did not come in, but stood with the door in his hand.

"One of the six, Tom, at last!" said Mr. Goodchild, in a surprised whisper. "Sir, your pleasure?"

"Sir, *your* pleasure?" said the one old man.

"I didn't ring."

"The bell did," said the one old man.

He said *bell*, in a deep strong way, that would have expressed the church bell.

"I had the pleasure, I believe, of seeing you, yesterday?" said Goodchild.

"I cannot undertake to say for certain," was the grim reply of the one old man.

"I think you saw me. Did you not?"

"Saw *you*?" said the old man. "Oh yes, I saw *you*. But, I see many who never see me."

A chilled, slow, earthy, fixed old man. A cadaverous old man of measured speech. An old man who seemed as unable to wink, as if his eyelids had been nailed to his forehead. An old man whose eyes—two spots of fire—had no more motion than if they had been connected with the back of his skull by screws driven through it, and riveted and bolted outside, among his grey hair.

The night had turned so cold, to Mr. Goodchild's sensations, that he shivered. He remarked lightly, and half apologetically, "I think somebody is walking over my grave."

"No," said the weird old man, "there is no one there."

Mr. Goodchild looked at Idle, but Idle lay with his head enwreathed in smoke.

"No one there?" said Goodchild.

"There is no one at your grave, I assure you," said the old man.

He had come in and shut the door, and he now sat down. He did not bend himself to sit, as other people do, but seemed to sink bolt upright, as if in water, until the chair stopped him.

"My friend, Mr. Idle," said Goodchild, extremely anxious to introduce a third person into the conversation.

"I am," said the old man, without looking at him, "at Mr. Idle's service."

"If you are an old inhabitant of this place," Francis Goodchild resumed.

"Yes."

"Perhaps you can decide a point my friend and I were in doubt upon, this morning. They hang condemned criminals at the castle, I believe?"

"*I* believe so," said the old man.

"Are their faces turned towards that noble prospect?"

"Your face is turned," replied the old man, "to the castle wall. When you are tied up, you see its stones expanding and contracting violently, and a similar expansion and contraction seem to take place in your own head and breast. Then, there is a rush of fire and an earthquake, and the castle springs into the air, and you tumble down a precipice."

His cravat appeared to trouble him. He put his hand to his throat, and moved his neck from side to side. He was an old man of a swollen character of face, and his nose was immovably hitched up on one side, as if by a little hook inserted in that nostril. Mr. Goodchild felt exceedingly uncomfortable, and began to think the night was hot, and not cold.

"A strong description, sir," he observed.

"A strong sensation," the old man rejoined.

Again, Mr. Goodchild looked to Mr. Thomas Idle; but Thomas lay on his back with his face attentively turned towards the one old man, and made no sign. At this time Mr. Goodchild believed that he saw threads of fire stretch from the old man's eyes to his own, and there attach themselves. (Mr. Goodchild writes the present account of his experience, and, with the utmost solemnity, protests that he had the strongest sensation upon him of being forced to look at the old man along those two fiery films, from that moment.)

"I must tell it to you," said the old man, with a ghastly and a stony stare.

"What?" asked Francis Goodchild.

"You know where it took place. Yonder!"

Whether he pointed to the room above, or to the room below, or to any room in that old house, or to a room in some other old house in that old town, Mr. Goodchild was not, nor is, nor ever can be, sure. He was confused by the circumstance that the right forefinger of the one old man seemed to dip itself in one of the threads of fire, light itself, and make a fiery start in the air, as it pointed somewhere. Having pointed somewhere, it went out.

"You know she was a bride," said the old man.

"I know they still send up bride cake," Mr. Goodchild faltered. "This is a very oppressive air."

She was a bride, said the old man. She was a fair, flaxen-haired, large-eyed girl, who had no character, no purpose. A weak, credulous, incapable, helpless nothing. Not like her mother. No, no. It was her father whose character she reflected.

Her mother had taken care to secure everything to herself, for her own life, when the father of this girl (a child at that time) died—of sheer helplessness; no other disorder—and then he renewed the acquaintance that had once subsisted between the mother and him. He had been put aside for the flaxen-haired, large-eyed man (or nonentity) with money. He could overlook that for money. He wanted compensation in money.

So, he returned to the side of that woman the mother, danced attendance on her, and submitted himself to her whims. She wreaked upon him every she had, or could invent. He bore it. And the more he bore, the more he wanted compensation in money, and the more he was resolved to have it.

But, lo! Before he got it, she cheated him. In one of her imperious states, she froze, and never thawed again. She put her hands to her head one night, uttered a cry, stiffened, lay in that attitude certain hours, and died. And he had got no compensation from her in money, yet. Blight and Murrain on her! Not a penny.

He had hated her throughout that second pursuit, and had longed for retaliation on her. He now counterfeited her signature to an instrument, leaving all she had to leave, to her daughter—ten years old then—to whom the property passed absolutely, and appointing himself the daughter's Guardian. When he slid it under the pillow of the bed on which she lay, he bent down in the deaf ear of Death, and whispered: "Mistress Pride, I have determined a long time that, dead or alive, you must make me compensation in money."

So, now there were only two left. Which two were, he, and the fair flaxen-haired, large-eyed foolish daughter, who afterwards became the bride.

He put her to school. In a secret, dark, oppressive, ancient house, he put her to school with a watchful and unscrupulous woman. "My worthy lady," he said, "here is a mind to be formed; will you help me to form it?" She accepted the trust. For which she, too, wanted compensation in money, and had it.

The girl was formed in the fear of him, and in the conviction, that there was no escape from him.

She was taught, from the first, to regard him as her future husband—the man who must marry her—the destiny that overshadowed her—the appointed certainty that could never be evaded. The poor fool was soft white wax in their hands, and took the impression that they put upon her. It hardened with time. It became a part of herself. Inseparable from herself, and only to be torn away from her, by tearing life away from her.

Eleven years she had lived in the dark house and its gloomy garden. He was jealous of the very light and air getting to her, and they kept her close. He stopped the wide chimneys, shaded the little windows, left the strong-stemmed ivy to wander where it would over the house-front, the moss to accumulate on the untrimmed fruit trees in the red-walled garden, the weeds to overrun its green and yellow walks. He surrounded her with images of sorrow and desolation. He caused her to be filled with fears of the place and of the stories that were told of it, and then on pretext of correcting them, to be left in it in solitude, or made to shrink about it in the dark. When her mind was most depressed and fullest of terrors, then, he would come out of one of the hiding places from which he overlooked her, and present himself as her sole resource.

Thus, by being from her childhood the one embodiment her life presented to her of power to coerce and power to relieve, power to bind and power to loose, the ascendency over her weakness was secured. She was twenty-one years and twenty-one days old, when he brought her home to the gloomy house, his half-witted, frightened, and submissive bride of three weeks.

He had dismissed the governess by that time—what he had left to do, he could best do alone—and they came back, upon a rainy night, to the scene of her long preparation. She turned to him upon the threshold, as the rain was dripping from the porch, and said, "Oh sir, it is the Deathwatch ticking for me!"

"Well!" he answered. "And if it were?"

"Oh sir!" she returned to him, "look kindly on me, and be merciful to me! I beg your pardon. I will do anything you wish, if you will only forgive me!"

That had become the poor fool's constant song: "I beg your pardon," and "Forgive me!"

She was not worth hating; he felt nothing but contempt for her. But, she had long been in the way, and he had long been weary, and the work was near its end, and had to be worked out.

"You fool," he said. "Go up the stairs!"

She obeyed very quickly, murmuring, "I will do anything you wish!" When he came into the bride's chamber, having been a little retarded by the heavy fastenings of the great door (for they were alone in the house, and he had arranged that the people who attended on them should come and go in the day), he found her withdrawn to the furthest corner, and there standing pressed against the paneling as if she would have shrunk through it: her flaxen hair all wild about her face, and her large eyes staring at him in vague terror.

"What are you afraid of? Come and sit down by me."

"I will do anything you wish. I beg your pardon, sir. Forgive me!" Her monotonous tune as usual.

"Ellen, here is a writing that you must write out tomorrow, in your own hand. You may as well be seen by others, busily engaged upon it. When you have written it all fairly, and corrected all mistakes, call in any two people there may be about the house, and sign your name to it before them. Then, put it in your pillow to keep it safe, and when I sit here again tomorrow night, give it to me."

"I will do it all, with the greatest care. I will do anything you wish."

"Don't shake and tremble, then."

"I will try my utmost not to do it—if you will only forgive me!"

Next day, she sat down at her desk, and did as she had been told. He often passed in and out of the room, to observe her, and always saw her slowly and laboriously writing: repeating to herself the words she copied, in appearance quite mechanically, and without caring or endeavoring to comprehend them, so that she did her task. He saw her follow the directions she had received, in all particulars; and at night, when they were alone again in the same bride's chamber, and he drew his chair to the hearth, she timidly approached him from her distant seat, took the paper from her pillow, and gave it into his hand.

It secured all her possessions to him, in the event of her death. He put her before him, face to face, that he might look at her steadily; and he asked her, in so many plain words, neither fewer nor more, did she know that?

There were spots of ink upon her white dress, and they made her face look whiter and her eyes look larger as she nodded her head. There were spots of ink upon the hand with which she stood before him, nervously plaiting and folding her white skirts.

He took her by the arm, and looked her, yet more closely and steadily, in the face. "Now, die! I have done with you."

She shrunk, and uttered a low, suppressed cry.

"I am not going to kill you. I will not endanger my life for yours. Die!"

He sat before her in the gloomy bride's chamber, day after day, night after night, looking the word at her when he did not utter it. As often as her large unmeaning eyes were raised from the hands in which she rocked her head, to the stern figure, sitting with crossed arms and knitted forehead, in the chair, they read in it, "Die!" When she dropped asleep in exhaustion, she was called back to shuddering consciousness, by the whisper, "Die!" When she fell upon her old entreaty to be pardoned, she was answered, "Die!" When she had outwatched and outsuffered the long night, and the rising sun flamed into the somber room, she heard it hailed with, "Another day and not dead? Die!"

Shut up in the deserted mansion, aloof from all mankind, and engaged alone in such a struggle without any respite, it came to this—that either he must die, or she. He knew it very well, and concentrated his strength against her feebleness. Hours upon hours he held her by the arm when her arm was black where he held it, and bade her Die!

It was done, upon a windy morning, before sunrise. He computed the time to be half-past four;

but, his forgotten watch had run down, and he could not be sure. She had broken away from him in the night, with loud and sudden cries—the first of that kind to which she had given vent—and he had had to put his hands over her mouth. Since then, she had been quiet in the corner of the paneling where she had sunk down; and he had left her, and had gone back with his folded arms and his knitted forehead to his chair.

Paler in the pale light, more colorless than ever in the leaden dawn, he saw her coming, trailing herself along the floor towards him—a white wreck of hair, and dress, and wild eyes, pushing itself on by an irresolute and bending hand.

"Oh, forgive me! I will do anything. Oh, sir, pray tell me I may live!"

"Die!"

"Are you so resolved? Is there no hope for me?"

"Die!"

Her large eyes strained themselves with wonder and fear; wonder and fear changed to reproach; reproach to blank nothing. It was done. He was not at first so sure it was done, but that the morning sun was hanging jewels in her hair—he saw the diamond, emerald, and ruby, glittering among it in little points, as he stood looking down at her—when he lifted her and laid her on her bed.

She was soon laid in the ground. And now they were all gone, and he had compensated himself well.

He had a mind to travel. Not that he meant to waste his money, for he was a pinching man and liked his money dearly (like nothing else, indeed), but, that he had grown tired of the desolate house and wished to turn his back upon it and have done with it. But, the house was worth money, and money must not be thrown away. He determined to sell it before he went. That it might look the less wretched and bring a better price, he hired some laborers to work in the overgrown garden; to cut out the dead wood, trim the ivy that drooped in heavy masses over the windows and gables, and clear the walks in which the weeds were growing mid-leg high.

He worked, himself, along with them. He worked later than they did, and one evening at dusk, was left working alone, with his billhook in his hand. One autumn evening, when the bride was five weeks dead.

"It grows too dark to work longer," he said to himself, "I must give over for the night."

He detested the house, and was loath to enter it. He looked at the dark porch waiting for him like a tomb, and felt that it was an accursed house. Near to the porch, and near to where he stood, was a tree whose branches waved before the old bay window of the bride's chamber, where it had been done. The tree swung suddenly, and made him start. It swung again, although the night was still. Looking up into it, he saw a figure among the branches.

It was the figure of a young man. The face looked down, as his looked up; the branches cracked and swayed; the figure rapidly descended, and slid upon its feet before him. A slender youth of about her age, with long light brown hair.

"What thief are you?" he said, seizing the youth by the collar.

The young man, in shaking himself free, swung him a blow with his arm across the face and throat.

They closed, but the young man got from him and stepped back, crying, with great eagerness and horror, "Don't touch me! I would as lief be touched by the Devil!"

He stood still, with his billhook in his hand, looking at the young man. For, the young man's look was the counterpart of her last look, and he had not expected ever to see that again.

"I am no thief. Even if I were, I would not have a coin of your wealth, if it would buy me the Indies. You murderer!"

"What!"

"I climbed it," said the young man, pointing up into the tree, "for the first time, nigh four years ago. I climbed it, to look at her. I saw her. I spoke to her. I have climbed it, many a time, to watch and listen for her. I was a boy, hidden among its leaves, when from that bay window she gave me this!"

He showed a tress of flaxen hair, tied with a mourning ribbon.

"Her life," said the young man, "was a life of mourning. She gave me this, as a token of it, and a sign that she was dead to everyone but you. If I had been older, if I had seen her sooner, I might have saved her from you. But, she was fast in the web when I first climbed the tree, and what could I do then to break it!"

In saying these words, he burst into a fit of sobbing and crying: weakly at first, then passionately, "Murderer! I climbed the tree on the night when you brought her back. I heard her, from the tree, speak of the Deathwatch at the door. I was three times in the tree while you were shut up with her, slowly killing her. I saw her, from the tree, lie dead upon her bed. I have watched you, from the tree, for proofs and traces of your guilt. The manner of it is a mystery to me yet, but I will pursue you until you have rendered up your life to the hangman. You shall never, until then, be rid of me. I loved her! I can know no relenting towards you. Murderer, I loved her!"

The youth was bareheaded, his hat having fluttered away in his descent from the tree. He moved towards the gate. He had to pass—him—to get to it. There was breadth for two old-fashioned carriages abreast; and the youth's abhorrence, openly expressed in every feature of his face and limb of his body, and very hard to bear, had verge enough to keep itself at a distance in. He (by which I mean the other) had not stirred hand or foot, since he had stood still to look at the boy. He faced round, now, to follow him with his eyes. As the back of the bare light brown head was turned to him, he saw a red curve stretch from his hand to it. He knew, before he threw the billhook, where it had alighted—I say, had alighted, and not would alight; for, to his clear perception the thing was done before he did it. It cleft the head, and it remained there, and the boy lay on his face.

He buried the body in the night, at the foot of a tree. As soon as it was light in the morning, he worked at turning up all the ground near the tree, and hacking and hewing at the neighboring bushes and undergrowth. When the laborers came, there was nothing suspicious, and nothing suspected.

But, he had, in a moment, defeated all his precautions, and destroyed the triumph of the scheme he had so long concerted, and so successfully worked out. He had got rid of the bride, and had acquired her fortune without endangering his life; but now, for a death by which he had gained nothing he had evermore to live with a rope around his neck.

Beyond this, he was chained to the house of gloom and horror, which he could not endure. Being afraid to sell it or to quit it, lest discovery should be made, he was forced to live in it. He hired two old people, man and wife, for his servants; and dwelled in it, and dreaded it. His great difficulty, for a long time, was the garden. Whether he should keep it trim, whether he should suffer it to fall into its former state of neglect, what would be least likely way of attracting attention to it?

He took the middle course of gardening, himself, in his evening leisure, and of then calling the old serving man to help him; but, of never letting him work there alone. And he made himself an arbor over against the tree, where he could sit and see it was safe.

As the seasons changed, and the tree changed, his mind perceived dangers that were always changing. In the leafy time, he perceived that the upper boughs were growing into the form of the young man—that they made the shape of him exactly, sitting in a forked branch swinging in the wind. In the time of the falling leaves, he perceived that they came down from the tree, forming telltale letters on the path, or that they had a tendency to heap themselves into a churchyard mound above the grave. In the winter, when the trees were bare, he perceived that the boughs swung at him the ghost of the blow the young man had given, and that they threatened him openly. In the spring, when the sap was mounting in the trunk, he asked himself, were the dried-up particles of blood mounting with it: to make out more obviously this year than last, the leaf-screened figure of the young man, swinging in the wind?

However, he turned his money over and over, and still over. He was in the dark trade, and gold dust trade, and most secret trades that yielded great returns. In ten years, he had turned his money over, so many times, that the traders and shippers who had dealings with him, absolutely did not lie—for once—when they declared that he had increased his fortune, twelve hundred per cent.

He possessed his riches one hundred years ago, when people could be lost easily. He had heard who the youth was, from hearing of the search that was made after him; but, it died away, and the youth was forgotten.

The annual round of changes in the tree had been repeated ten times since the night of the burial at its foot, when there was a great thunderstorm over this place. It broke at midnight, and raged until morning. The first intelligence he heard from his old serving man that morning, was, that the tree had been struck by lightning.

It had been driven down the stem, in a very surprising manner, and the stem lay in two blighted shafts: one resting against the house, and one against a portion of the old red garden wall in which its fall had made a gap. The fissure went down the tree to a little above the earth, and there stopped. There was great curiosity to see the tree, and, with most of his former fears revived, he sat in his arbor—grown quite an old man—watching the people who came to see it.

They quickly began to come, in such dangerous numbers, that he closed his garden gate and refused to admit any more. But, there were certain men of science who traveled from a distance to examine the tree, and, in an evil hour, he let them in—Blight and Murrain on them, let them in!

They wanted to dig up the ruin by the roots, and closely examine it, and the earth about it. Never, while he lived! They offered money for it. They! Men of science, whom he could have bought by the gross, with a scratch of his pen! He showed them the garden gate again, and locked and barred it.

But they were bent on doing what they wanted to do, and they bribed the old serving man—a thankless wretch who regularly complained when he received his wages, of being underpaid—and they stole into the garden by night with their lanterns, picks, and shovels, and fell to at the tree. He was lying in a turret room on the other side of the house (the bride's chamber had been unoccupied ever since), but he soon dreamed of picks and shovels, and got up.

He came to an upper window on that side, whence he could see their lanterns, and them, and the loose earth in a heap which he had himself disturbed and put back, when it was last turned to the air. It was found! They had that minute lighted on it. They were all bending over it. One of them said, "The skull is fractured"; and another, "See here the bones"; and another, "See here the clothes"; and then the first struck in again, and said, "A rusty billhook!"

He became sensible, next day, that he was already put under strict watch, and that he could go nowhere without being followed. Before a week was out, he was taken and laid in hold. The circumstances were gradually pieced together against him, with a desperate malignity, and an appalling ingenuity. But, see the justice of men, and how it was extended to him! He was further accused of having poisoned that girl in the bride's chamber. He, who had carefully and expressly avoided imperiling a hair of his head for her, and who had seen her die of her own incapacity!

There was doubt for which of the two murders he should be first tried; but, the real one was chosen, and he was found guilty, and cast for death. Bloodthirsty wretches! They would have made him guilty of anything, so set they were upon having his life.

His money could do nothing to save him, and he was hanged. *I* am he, and I was hanged at Lancaster Castle with my face to the wall, a hundred years ago!

At this terrific announcement, Mr. Goodchild tried to rise and cry out. But, the two fiery lines extending from the old man's eyes to his own, kept him down, and he could not utter a sound. His sense of hearing, however, was acute, and he could hear the clock strike two. No sooner had he heard the clock strike Two, than he saw before him two old men!

Two.

The eyes of each, connected with his eyes by two films of fire: each, exactly like the other: each, addressing him at precisely one and the same instant: each, gnashing the same teeth in the same head, with the same twitched nostril above them, and the same suffused expression around it. Two old men. Differing in nothing, equally distinct to the sight, the copy no fainter than the original, the second as real as the first.

"At what time," said the two old men, "did you arrive at the door below?"

"At six."

"And there were six old men upon the stairs!"

Mr. Goodchild having wiped the perspiration from his brow, or tried to do it, the two old men proceeded in one voice, and in the singular number:

I had been anatomized, but had not yet had my skeleton put together and rehung on an iron hook, when it began to be whispered that the bride's chamber was haunted. It *was* haunted, and I was there.

We were there. She and I were there. I, in the chair upon the hearth; she, a white wreck again, trailing itself towards me on the floor. But, I was the speaker no more, and the one word that she said to me from midnight until dawn was, "Live!"

The youth was there, likewise. In the tree outside the window. Coming and going in the moonlight, as the tree bent and gave. He has, ever since, been there, peeping in at me in my torment; revealing to me by snatches, in the pale lights and slaty shadows where he comes and goes, bareheaded—a billhook, standing edgewise in his hair.

In the bride's chamber, every night from midnight until dawn—one month in the year expected, as I am going to tell you—he hides in the tree, and she comes towards me on the floor; always approaching; never coming nearer; always visible as if by moonlight, whether the moon shines or no; always saying, from midnight until dawn, her one word, "Live!"

But, in the month wherein I was forced out of this life—this present month of thirty days—the bride's chamber is empty and quiet. Not so my old dungeon. Not so the rooms where I was restless and afraid, ten years. Both are fitfully haunted then. At one in the morning, I am what you saw me when the clock struck that hour—one old man. At two in the morning, I am two old men. At three, I am three. By twelve at noon, I am twelve old men, one for every hundred per cent of old gain. Every one of the twelve, with twelve at night, I, twelve old men in anguish and fearful foreboding, wait for the coming of the executioner. At twelve at night, I, twelve old men turned off, swing invisible outside Lancaster Castle, with twelve faces to the wall!

When the bride's chamber was first haunted, it was known to me that this punishment would never cease, until I could make its nature, and my story, known to two living men together. I waited for the coming of two living men together into the bride's chamber, years upon years. It was infused into my knowledge (of the means I am ignorant) that if two living men, with their eyes open, could be in the bride's chamber at one in the morning, they would see me sitting in my chair.

At length, the whispers that the room was spiritually troubled, brought two men to try the adventure. I was scarcely struck upon the hearth at midnight (I came there as if the lightning blasted me into being), when I heard them ascending the stairs. Next, I saw them enter. One of them was a bold, active man, in the prime of life, some five and forty years of age; the other, a dozen years younger. They brought provisions with them in a basket, and bottles. A young woman accompanied them, with wood and coals for the lighting of the fire. When she had lighted it, the bold, active man accompanied her along the gallery outside the room, to see her safely down the staircase, and came back laughing.

He locked the door, examined the chamber, put out the contents of the basket on the table before the fire—little knowing of me, in my appointed station on the hearth, close to him—and filled the glasses, and ate and drank. His companion did the same, and was as cheerful and confident as he: though he was the leader. When they had supped, they laid pistols on the table, turned to the fire, and began to smoke their pipes of foreign make.

They had traveled together, and had been much together, and had an abundance of subjects in common. In the midst of their talking and laughing, the younger man made a reference to the leader's being always ready for any adventure; that one, or any other. He replied in these words: "Not quite so, Dick; if I am afraid of nothing else, I am afraid of myself."

His companion, seeming to grow a little dull, asked him, in what sense? How?

"Why, thus," he returned. "Here is a Ghost to be disproved. Well! I cannot answer for what my fancy might do if I were alone here, or what tricks my senses might play with me if they had me to themselves. But, in company with another man, and especially with you, Dick, I would consent to outface all the ghosts that were ever told of in the universe.''

''I had not the vanity to suppose that I was of so much importance tonight,'' said the other.

''Of so much,'' rejoined the leader, more seriously than he had spoken yet, ''that I would, for the reason I have given, on no account have undertaken to pass the night here alone.''

It was within a few minutes of one. The head of the younger man had drooped when he made his last remark, and it drooped lower now.

''Keep awake, Dick!'' said the leader, gaily. ''The small hours are the worst.''

He tried, but his head drooped again.

''Dick!'' urged the leader. ''Keep awake!''

''I can't,'' he indistinctly muttered. ''I don't know what strange influence is stealing over me. I can't.''

His companion looked at him with a sudden horror, and I, in my different way, felt a new horror also; for, it was on the stroke of one, and I felt that the second watcher was yielding to me, and that the curse was upon me that I must send him to sleep.

''Get up and walk, Dick,'' cried the leader. ''Try!''

It was in vain to go behind the slumberer's chair and shake him. One o'clock sounded, and I was present to the elder man, and he stood transfixed before me.

To him alone, I was obliged to relate my story, without hope of benefit. To him alone, I was an awful phantom making a quite useless confession. I foresee it will ever be the same. The two living men together will never come to release me. When I appear, the senses of one of the two will be locked in sleep; he will neither see nor hear me; my communication will ever be made to a solitary listener, and will ever be unserviceable. Woe! Woe! Woe!

As the two old men, with these words, wrung their hands, it shot into Mr. Goodchild's mind that he was in the terrible situation of being virtually alone with the specter, and that Mr. Idle's immovability was explained by his having been charmed asleep at one o'clock. In the terror of this sudden discovery which produced an indescribable dread, he struggled so hard to get free from the four fiery threads, that he snapped them, after he had pulled them out to a great width. Being then out of bonds, he caught up Mr. Idle from the sofa and rushed downstairs with him.

"What are you about, Francis?" demanded Mr. Idle. "My bedroom is not down here. What the deuce are you carrying me at all for? I can walk with a stick now. I don't want to be carried. Put me down."

Mr. Goodchild put him down in the old hall, and looked about him wildly.

"What are you doing? Idiotically plunging at your own friends, and rescuing them or perishing in the attempt?" asked Mr. Idle, in a highly petulant state.

"The one old man!" cried Mr. Goodchild, distractedly, "and the two old men!"

Mr. Idle deigned no other reply than, "The one

old woman, I think you mean," as he began hobbling his way back up the staircase, with the assistance of its broad balustrade.

"I assure you, Tom," began Mr. Goodchild, attending at his side, "that since you fell asleep—"

"Come, I like that!" said Thomas Idle. "I haven't closed an eye!"

With the peculiar sensitiveness on the subject of the disgraceful action of going to sleep out of bed, which is the lot of all mankind, Mr. Idle persisted in this declaration. The same peculiar sensitiveness impelled Mr. Goodchild, on being taxed with the same crime, to repudiate it with honorable resentment. The settlement of the question of the one old man and the two old men was thus presently complicated, and soon made quite impracticable. Mr. Idle said it was all bride cake, and fragments, newly arranged, of things seen and thought about in the day. Mr. Goodchild said how could that be, when he hadn't been asleep, and what right could Mr. Idle have to say so, who had been asleep? Mr. Idle said he had never been asleep, and never did go to sleep, and that Mr. Goodchild, as a general rule, was always asleep. They consequently parted for the rest of the night, at their bedroom doors, a little ruffled. Mr. Goodchild's last words were, that he had had, in that real and tangible old sitting room of that real and tangible old Inn (he supposed Mr. Idle denied its existence?), every sensation and experience, the present record of which is now within a line or two of completion; and that he could write it out and print it every word. Mr. Idle returned that he might if he liked—and he did like, and has now done it.

Sir Arthur Conan Doyle

The Adventure of the Norwood Builder

"From the point of view of the criminal expert," said Mr. Sherlock Holmes, "London has become a singularly uninteresting city since the death of the late lamented Professor Moriarty."

"I can hardly think that you would find many decent citizens to agree with you," I answered.

"Well, well, I must not be selfish," said he, with a smile, as he pushed back his chair from the breakfast table. "The community is certainly the gainer, and no one the loser, save the poor-out-of-work specialist, whose occupation has gone. With that man in the field, one's morning paper presented infinite possibilites. Often it was only the smallest trace, Watson, the faintest indication, and yet it was enough to tell me that the great malignant brain was there, as the gentlest tremors of the edges of the web remind one of the foul spider which lurks in the center. Petty thefts, wanton assaults, purposeless outrage—to the man who held the clue all could be worked into one connected whole. To the scientific student of the higher criminal world, no capital in Europe offered the advantages which London then possessed. But now—" He shrugged his shoulders in humorous deprecation of the state of things which he had himself done so much to produce.

At the time of which I speak, Holmes had been back for some months, and I at his request had sold my practice and returned to share the old quarters in Baker Street. A young doctor, named Verner, had purchased my small Kensington practice, and given with astonishingly little demur the highest price that I ventured to ask—an incident which only explained itself some years later, when I found that Verner was a distant relation of Holmes, and that it was my friend who had really found the money.

Our months of partnership had not been so uneventful as he had stated, for I find, on looking over my notes, that this period includes the case of the papers of ex-President Murillo, and also the shocking affair of the Dutch steamship *Friesland*, which so nearly cost us both our lives. His cold and proud nature was always averse, however, from anything in the shape of public applause, and he bound me in the most stringent terms to say no further word of himself, his methods, or his success—a prohibition which, as I have explained, has only now been removed.

Mr. Sherlock Holmes was leaning back in his chair after his whimsical protest, and was unfolding his morning paper in a leisurely fashion, when our attention was arrested by a tremendous ring at the bell, followed immediately by a hollow drumming sound, as if someone were beating on the outer door with his fist. As it opened there came a tumultuous rush into the hall, rapid feet clattered up the stair, and an instant later a wild-eyed and frantic young man, pale, disheveled, and palpitating, burst into the room. He looked from one to the other of us, and under our gaze of inquiry he became conscious that some apology was needed for this unceremonious entry.

"I'm sorry, Mr. Holmes," he cried. "You mustn't blame me. I am nearly mad. Mr. Holmes, I am the unhappy John Hector McFarlane."

He made the announcement as if the name alone would explain both his visit and its manner, but I could see, by my companion's unresponsive face, that it meant no more to him than to me.

"Have a cigarette, Mr. McFarlane," said he, pushing his case across. "I am sure that, with your symptoms, my friend Dr. Watson here would prescribe a sedative. The weather has been so very warm these last few days. Now, if you feel a little more composed, I should be glad if you would sit down in that chair, and tell us very slowly and quietly who you are, and what it is that you want. You mentioned your name, as if I should recognize it, but I assure you that, beyond the obvious facts that you are a bachelor, a solicitor, a Freemason, and an asthmatic, I know nothing whatever about you."

Familiar as I was with my friend's methods, it was not difficult for me to follow his deductions, and to observe the untidiness of attire, the sheaf of legal papers, the watch-charm, and the breathing which had prompted them. Our client, however, stared in amazement.

"Yes, I am all that, Mr. Holmes; and, in addition, I am the most unfortunate man at this moment in London. For heaven's sake, don't abandon me, Mr. Holmes! If they come to arrest me before I have finished my story, make them give me time, so that I may tell you the whole truth. I could go to jail happy if I knew that you were working for me outside."

"Arrest you!" said Holmes. "This is really most grati—most interesting. On what charge do you expect to be arrested?"

"Upon the charge of murdering Mr. Jonas Oldacre, of Lower Norwood."

My companion's expressive face showed a sympathy which was not, I am afraid, entirely unmixed with satisfaction.

"Dear me," said he, "it was only this moment at breakfast that I was saying to my friend, Dr. Watson, that sensational cases had disappeared out of our papers."

Our visitor stretched forward a quivering hand and picked up the *Daily Telegraph*, which still lay upon Holmes's knee.

"If you had looked at it, sir, you would have seen at a glance what the errand is on which I have come to you this morning. I feel as if my name and misfortune must be in every man's mouth." He turned it over to expose the central page. "Here it is, and with your permission I will read it to you. Listen to this, Mr. Holmes. The headlines are: 'Mysterious Affair at Lower Norwood. Disappearance of a Well-Known Builder. Suspicion of

Murder and Arson. A Clue to the Criminal.' That is the clue which they are already following, Mr. Holmes, and I know that it leads infallibly to me. I have been followed from London Bridge Station, and I am sure that they are only waiting for the warrant to arrest me. It will break my mother's heart—it will break her heart!" He wrung his hands in an agony of apprehension, and swayed backward and forward in his chair.

I looked with interest upon this man, who was accused of being the perpetrator of a crime of violence. He was flaxen-haired and handsome, in a washed-out negative fashion, with frightened blue eyes, and a clean-shaven face, with a weak, sensitive mouth. His age may have been about twenty-seven, his dress and bearing that of a gentleman. From the pocket of his light summer overcoat protruded the bundle of endorsed papers which proclaimed his profession.

"We must use what time we have," said Holmes. "Watson, would you have the kindness to take the paper and to read the paragraph in question?"

Underneath the vigorous headlines which our client had quoted, I read the following suggestive narrative:

"Late last night, or early this morning, an incident occurred at Lower Norwood which points, it is feared, to a serious crime. Mr. Jonas Oldacre is a well-known resident of that suburb, where he has carried on his business as a builder for many years. Mr. Oldacre is a bachelor, fifty-two years of age, and lives in Deep Dene House, at the Sydenham end of the road of that name. He has had the reputation of being a man of eccentric habits, secretive and retiring. For some years he has practically withdrawn from the business, in which he is said to have massed considerable wealth. A small timber yard still exists, however, at the back of the house, and last night, about twelve o'clock, an alarm was given that one of the stacks was on fire. The engines were soon upon the spot, but the dry wood burned with great fury, and it was impossible to arrest the conflagration until the stack had been entirely consumed. Up to this point the incident bore the appearance of an ordinary accident, but fresh indications seem to point to the serious crime. Surprise was expressed at the absence of the master of the establishment from the scene of the fire, and an inquiry followed, which showed that he had disappeared from the house. An examination of his room revealed that the bed had not been slept in, that a safe which stood in it was open, that a number of important papers were scattered about the room, and finally, that there were signs of a murderous struggle, slight traces of blood being found within the room, and an oaken walking stick, which also showed stains of blood upon the handle. It is known that Mr. Jonas Oldacre had received a late visitor in his bedroom upon that night, and the stick found has been identified as the property of this person, who is a young London solicitor named John Hector McFarlane, junior partner of Graham and McFarlane, of 426 Gresham Buildings, E.C. The police believe that they have evidence in their possession which supplies a very convincing motive for the crime, and altogether it cannot be doubted that sensational developments will follow.

"LATER.—It is rumored as we go to press that Mr. John Hector McFarlane has actually been arrested on the charge of the murder of Mr. Jonas Oldacre. It is at least certain that a warrant has been issued. There have been further and sinister developments in the investigation at Norwood. Besides the signs of a struggle in the room of the unfortunate builder it is now known that the French windows of his bedroom (which is on the ground floor) were found to be open, that there were marks as if some bulky object had been dragged across the woodpile, and, finally, it is asserted that charred remains have been found among the charcoal ashes of the fire. The police theory is that a most sensational crime has been committed, that the victim was clubbed to death in his own bedroom, his papers rifled, and his dead body dragged across to the woodstack, which was then ignited so as to hide all traces of the crime. The conduct of the criminal investigation has been left in the experienced hands of Inspector Lestrade, of Scotland Yard, who is following up the clues with his accustomed energy and sagacity."

Sherlock Holmes listened with closed eyes and fingertips together to this remarkable account.

"The case has certainly some points of interest," said he, in his languid fashion. "May I ask, in the first place, Mr. McFarlane, how it is that you are still at liberty, since there appears to be enough evidence to justify your arrest?"

"I live at Torrington Lodge, Blackheath, with my parents, Mr. Holmes, but last night, having to do business very late with Mr. Jonas Oldacre, I stayed at a hotel in Norwood, and came to my business from there. I knew nothing of this affair until I was in the train, when I read what you have just heard. I at once saw the horrible danger of my position, and I hurried to put the case into your hands. I have no doubt that I should have been arrested either at my city office or at my home. A man followed me from London Bridge Station, and I have no doubt—Great heaven! What is that?"

It was a clang of the bell, followed instantly by heavy steps upon the stair. A moment later, our old friend Lestrade appeared in the doorway. Over his shoulder I caught a glimpse of one or two uniformed policemen outside.

"Mr. John Hector McFarlane?" said Lestrade.

Our unfortunate client rose with a ghastly face.

"I arrest you for the wilful murder of Mr. Jonas Oldacre, of Lower Norwood."

McFarlane turned to us with a gesture of despair, and sank into his chair once more like one who is crushed.

"One moment, Lestrade," said Holmes. "Half an hour more or less can make no difference to you, and the gentleman was about to give us an account of this very interesting affair, which might aid us in clearing it up."

"I think there will be no difficulty in clearing it up," said Lestrade, grimly.

"Nonetheless, with your permission, I should be most interested to hear his account."

"Well, Mr. Holmes, it is difficult for me to refuse you anything, for you have been of use to the force one or twice in the past, and we owe you a good turn at Scotland Yard," said Lestrade. "At the same time I must remain with my prisoner, and

I am bound to warn him that anything he may say will appear in evidence against him."

"I wish nothing better," said our client. "All I ask is that you should hear and recognize the absolute truth."

Lestrade looked at his watch. "I'll give you half an hour," said he.

"I must explain first," said McFarlane, "that I knew nothing of Mr. Jonas Oldacre. His name was familiar to me, for many years ago my parents were acquainted with him, but they drifted apart. I was very much surprised, therefore, when yesterday, about three o'clock in the afternoon, he walked into my office in the city. But I was still more astonished when he told me the object of his visit. He had in his hand several sheets of a notebook, covered with scribbled writing—here they are—and he laid them on my table.

" 'Here is my will," he said. "I want you, Mr. McFarlane, to cast it into proper legal shape. I will sit here while you do so.'

"I set myself to copy it, and you can imagine my astonishment when I found that, with some reservations, he had left all his property to me. He was a strange little ferret-like man, with white eyelashes, and when I looked up at him I found his keen gray eyes fixed upon me with an amused expression. I could hardly believe my own senses as I read the terms of the will; but he explained that he was a bachelor with hardly any living relation, that he had known my parents in his youth, and that he had always heard of me as a very deserving young man, and was assured that his money would be in worthy hands. Of course, I could only stammer out my thanks. The will was duly finished, signed, and witnessed by my clerk. This is it on the blue paper, and those slips, as I have explained, are the rough draft. Mr. Jonas Oldacre then informed me that there were a number of documents—building leases, title deeds, mortgages, scrip, and so forth—which it was necessary that I should see and understand. He said that his mind would not be easy until the whole thing was settled, and he begged me to come out to his house at Norwood that night, bringing the will with me, and to arrange matters. 'Remember, my boy, not one word to your parents about the affair until everything is settled. We will keep it as a little surprise for them.' He was very insistent upon this point, and made me promise it faithfully.

"You can imagine, Mr. Holmes, that I was not in a humor to refuse him anything that he might ask. He was my benefactor, and all my desire was to carry out his wishes in every particular. I sent a telegram home, therefore, to say that I had important business on hand, and that it was impossible for me to say how late I might be. Mr. Oldacre had told me that he would like me to have supper with him at nine, as he might not be home before that hour. I had some difficulty in finding his house, however, and it was nearly half-past before I reached it. I found him—"

"One moment!" said Holmes. "Who opened the door?"

"A middle-aged woman, who was, I suppose, his housekeeper."

"And it was she, I presume, who mentioned your name?"

"Exactly," said McFarlane.

"Pray proceed."

McFarlane wiped his damp brow, and then continued his narrative:

"I was shown by this woman into a sitting room, where a frugal supper was laid out. Afterwards, Mr. Jonas Oldacre led me into his bedroom, in which there stood a heavy safe. This he opened and took out a mass of documents, which we went over together. It was between eleven and twelve when we finished. He remarked that we must not disturb the housekeeper. He showed me out through his own French window, which had been open all this time."

"Was the blind down?" asked Holmes.

"I will not be sure, but I believe that it was only half down. Yes, I remember how he pulled it up in order to swing open the window. I could not find my stick, and he said, "Never mind, my boy, I shall see a good deal of you now, I hope, and I will keep your stick until you come back to claim it." I left him there, the safe open, and the papers made up in packets upon the table. It was so late that I could not get back to Blackheath, so I spent the night at the Anerley Arms, and I knew nothing more until I read of this horrible affair in the morning."

"Anything more that you would like to ask, Mr. Holmes?" said Lestrade, whose eyebrows had gone up once or twice during this remarkable explanation.

"Not until I have been to Blackheath."

"You mean to Norwood," said Lestrade.

"Oh, yes, no doubt that is what I must have

meant," said Holmes, with his enigmatical smile. Lestrade had learned by more experiences that he would care to acknowledge that that razor-like brain could cut through that which was impenetrable to him. I saw him look curiously at my companion.

"I think I should like to have a word with you presently, Mr. Sherlock Holmes," said he. "Now, Mr. McFarlane, two of my constables are at the door, and there is a four-wheeler waiting." The wretched young man arose, and with a last beseeching glance at us walked from the room. The officers conducted him to the cab, but Lestrade remained.

Holmes had picked up the pages which formed the rough draft of the will, and was looking at them with the keenest interest upon his face.

"There are some points about that document, Lestrade, are there not?" said he, pushing them over.

The official looked at them with a puzzled expression.

"I can read the first few lines, and these in the middle of the second page, and one or two at the end. Those are as clear as print," said he, "but the writing in between is very bad, and there are three places where I cannot read it at all."

"What do you make of that?" said Holmes.

"Well, what do *you* make of it?"

"That it was written in a train. The good writing represents stations, the bad writing movement, and the very bad writing passing over points. A scientific expert would pronounce at once that this was drawn up on a suburban line, since nowhere save in the immediate vicinity of great city could there be so quick a succession of points. Granting that his whole journey was occupied in drawing up the will, then the train was an express, only stopping once between Norwood and London Bridge."

Lestrade began to laugh.

"You are too many for me when you begin to get on your theories, Mr. Holmes," said he. "How does this bear on the case?"

"Well, it corroborates the young man's story to the extent that the will was drawn up by Jonas Oldacre in his journey yesterday. It is curious—is it not?—that a man should draw up so important a document in so haphazard a fashion. It suggests that he did not think it was going to be of much practical importance. If a man drew up a will which he did not intend ever to be effective, he might do it so."

"Well, he drew up his own death warrant at the same time," said Lestrade.

"Oh, you think so?"

"Don't you?"

"Well, it is quite possible, but the case is not clear to me yet."

"Not clear? Well, if that isn't clear, what *could* be clear? Here is a young man who learns suddenly that, if a certain older man dies, he will succeed to a fortune. What does he do? He says nothing to anyone, but he arranges that he shall go out on some pretext to see his client that night. He waits until the only other person in the house is in bed, and then in the solitude of a man's room he murders him, burns his body in the woodpile, and departs to a neighboring hotel. The bloodstains in the room and also on the stick are very slight. It is probable that he imagined his crime to be a bloodless one, and hoped that if the body were consumed it would hide all traces of the method of his death—traces which, for some reason, must have pointed to him. Is not all this obvious?"

"It strikes me, my good Lestrade, as being just a trifle too obvious," said Holmes. "You do not add imagination to your other great qualities, but if you could for one moment put yourself in the place of this young man, would you choose the very night after the will had been made to commit your crime? Would it not seem dangerous to you to make so very close a relation between the two incidents? Again, would you choose an occasion when you are known to be in the house, when a servant has let you in? And, finally, would you take the great pains to conceal the body, and yet leave your own stick as a sign that you were the criminal? Confess, Lestrade, that all this is very unlikely."

"As to the stick, Mr. Holmes, you know as well as I do that a criminal is often flurried, and does such things, which a cool man would avoid. He was very likely afraid to go back to the room. Give me another theory that would fit the facts."

"I could very easily give you half a dozen," said Holmes. "Here, for example, is a very possible and even probable one. I make you a free present of it. The older man is showing documents which are of evident value. A passing tramp sees them through the window, the blind of which is only half down. Exit the solicitor. Enter the tramp! He seizes a stick, which he observes there, kills Oldacre, and departs after burning the body.''

''Why should the tramp burn the body?''

''For the matter of that, why should McFarlane?''

''To hide some evidence.''

''Possibly the tramp wanted to hide that any murder at all had been committed.''

''And why did the tramp take nothing?''

''Because they were papers that he could not negotiate.''

Lestrade shook his head, though it seemed to me that his manner was less absolutely assured than before.

''Well, Mr. Sherlock Holmes, you may look for your tramp, and while you are finding him we will hold on to our man. The future will show which is right. Just notice this point, Mr. Holmes: that so far as we know, none of the papers were removed, and that the prisoner is the one man in the world who had no reason for removing them, since he was heir-at-law, and would come into them in any case.''

My friend seemed struck by this remark.

''I don't mean to deny that the evidence is in some ways very strongly in favor of your theory,'' said he. ''I only wish to point out that there are other theories possible. As you say, the future will decide. Good morning! I dare say that in the course of the day I shall drop in at Norwood and see how you are getting on.''

When the detective departed, my friend rose and made his preparations for the day's work with the alert air of a man who has a congenial task before him.

"My first movement, Watson," said he, as he bustled into his frockcoat, "must, as I said, be in the direction of Blackheath."

"And why not Norwood!"

"Because we have in this case one singular incident coming close to the heels of another singular incident. The police are making the mistake of concentrating their attention upon the second, because it happens to be the one which is actually criminal. But it is evident to me that the logical way to approach the case is to begin by trying to throw some light upon the first incident—the curious will, so suddenly made, and to so unexpected an heir. It may do something to simplify what followed. No, my dear fellow, I don't think you can help me. There is no prospect of danger, or I should not dream of stirring out without you. I trust that when I see you in the evening, I will be able to report that I have been able to do something for this unfortunate youngster, who has thrown himself upon my protection."

It was late when my friend returned, and I could see, by a glance at his haggard and anxious face, that the high hopes with which he had started had not been fulfilled. For an hour he droned away upon his violin, endeavoring to soothe his own ruffled spirits. At last he flung down the instrument, and plunged into a detailed account of his misadventures.

"It's all going wrong, Watson—all as wrong as it can go. I kept a bold face before Lestrade, but, upon my soul, I believe that for once the fellow is on the right track and we are on the wrong. All my instincts are one way, and all the facts are the other, and I must fear that British juries have not yet attained that pitch of intelligence when they will give the preference to my theories over Lestrade's facts."

"Did you go to Blackheath?"

"Yes, Watson, I went there, and I found very quickly that the late lamented Oldacre was a pretty considerable blackguard. The father was away in search of his son. The mother was at home—a little, fluffy, blue-eyed person, in a tremor of fear and indignation. Of course, she would not admit even the possibility of his guilt. But she would not express either surprise or regret over the fate of Oldacre. On the contrary, she spoke of him with such bitterness that she was unconsciously considerably strengthening the case of the police for, of course, if her son had heard her speak of the man in this fashion, it would predispose him towards hatred and violence. 'He was more like a malignant and cunning ape than a human being,' said she, 'and he always was, ever since he was a young man.'

" 'You knew him at that time?' said I.

" 'Yes, I knew him well, in fact, he was an old suitor of mine. Thank heaven that I had the sense to turn away from him and to marry a better, if poorer, man. I was engaged to him, Mr. Holmes, when I heard a shocking story of how he had turned a cat loose in an aviary, and I was so horrified at his brutal cruelty that I would have nothing more to do with him.' She rummaged in a bureau, and presently she produced a photograph, of a woman, shamefully defaced and mutilated with a knife. "That is my own photograph,' she said. 'He sent it to me in that state, with his curse, upon my wedding morning.'

" 'Well,' said I, 'at least he has forgiven you now, since he has left all his property to your son.'

" 'Neither my son nor I want anything from Jonas Oldacre, dead or alive!' she cried, with a proper spirit. 'There is a God in heaven, Mr. Holmes, and that same God who has punished that wicked man will show, in His own good time, that my son's hands are guiltless of his blood.'

"Well, I tried one or two leads, but could get at nothing which would help our hypothesis, and several points which would make against it. I gave it up at last, and off I went to Norwood.

"This place, Deep Dene House, is a big modern villa of staring brick, standing back in its own grounds, with a laurel-clumped lawn in front of it. To the right and some distance back from the road was the timber yard which had been the scene of the fire. Here's a rough plan on a leaf of my notebook. This window on the left is the one which opens into Oldacre's room. You can look into it from the road, you see. That is about the only bit of consolation I have had today. Lestrade was not there, but his head constable did the honors. They had just found a great treasure trove. They had spent the morning raking among the ashes of the burned woodpile, and besides the charred organic remains they had secured several discolored metal discs. I examined them with care, and there was no doubt that they were trouser buttons. I even distinguished that one of them was marked with the name of 'Hyams,' who was Oldacre's tailor. I then worked the lawn very carefully for signs or traces, but this drought has made everything as hard as iron. Nothing was to be seen save that same body or bundle had been dragged through a low privet hedge which is in line with the woodpile. All that, of course, fits in with the official theory. I crawled about the lawn with an August sun on my back, but I got up at the end of an hour no wiser than before.

"Well, after this fiasco I went into the bedroom and examined that also. The bloodstains were very slight, mere smears and discolorations, but undoubtedly fresh. The stick had been removed, but there also the marks were slight. There is no doubt about the stick belonging to our client. He admits it. Footmarks of both men could be made out on the carpet, but none of any third person, which again is a trick for the other side. They were piling up their score all the time and we were at a standstill.

"Only one little gleam of hope did I get—and yet it amounted to nothing. I examined the contents of the safe, most of which had been taken out and left on the table. The papers had been made up into sealed envelopes, one or two of which had been opened by the police. They were not, so far as I could judge, of any great value, or did the bankbook show that Mr. Oldacre was in such very affluent circumstances. But it seemed to me that all the papers were not there. There were allusions to some deeds—possibly the more valuable—which I could not find. This of course, if we could definitely prove it, would turn Lestrade's argument against himself; for who would steal a thing if he knew that he would shortly inherit it?

"Finally, having drawn every other cover and picked up no scent, I tried my luck with the housekeeper, Mrs. Lexington is her name—a little, dark, silent person, with suspicious and sidelong eyes. She could tell us something if she would—I am convinced of it. But she was as close as wax. Yes, she had let Mr. McFarlane in at half-past nine. She wished her hand had withered before she had done so. She had gone to bed at half-past ten. Her room was at the other end of the house, and she could hear nothing of what passed. Mr. McFarlane had left his hat, and to the best of her belief his stick, in the hall. She had been awakened by the alarm of fire. Her poor, dear master had certainly been murdered. Had he any enemies? Well, every man had enemies, but Mr. Oldacre kept himself very much to himself, and only met people in the way of business. She had seen the buttons, and was sure that they belonged to the clothes which he had worn last night. The woodpile was very dry, for it had not rained for a month. It burned like tinder, and by the time she reached the spot, nothing could be seen but flames. She and all the firemen smelled the burned flesh from inside it. She knew nothing of the papers, nor of Mr. Oldacre's private affairs.

"So, my dear Watson, there's my report of a failure. And yet—and yet—" he clenched his thin hands in a paroxysm of conviction—"I *know* it's all wrong. I feel it in my bones. There is something that has not come out, and that housekeeper knows it. There was a sort of sulky defiance in her eyes, which only goes with guilty knowledge. However, there's no good talking anymore about it, Watson; but unless some lucky chance comes our way I fear that the Norwood Disappearance Case will not figure in that chronicle of our successes which I foresee that a patient public will sooner or later have to endure."

"Surely," said I, "the man's appearance would go far with any jury?"

"That is a dangerous argument, my dear Watson. You remember that terrible murderer, Bert Stevens, who wanted us to get him off in '87? Was there ever a more mild-mannered, Sunday school young man?"

"It is true."

"Unless we succeed in establishing an alternative theory, this man is lost: You can hardly find a flaw in the case which can now be presented against him, and all further investigation has served to strengthen it. By the way, there is one curious little point about those papers which may serve us as the starting point for an inquiry. On looking over the bankbook I found that the low state of the balance was principally due to large checks which have been made out during the last year to Mr. Cornelius. I confess that I should be interested to know who this Mr. Cornelius may be with whom a retired builder has had such very large transactions. Is it possible that he has had a hand in the affair? Cornelius might be a broker, but we have found no scrip to correspond with these large payments. Failing any other indication, my researches must now take the direction of an inquiry at the bank for the gentleman who has cashed these checks. But I fear, my dear fellow, that our case will end ingloriously by Lestrade hanging our client, which will certainly be a triumph for Scotland Yard."

I do not know how far Sherlock Holmes took any sleep that night, but when I came down to breakfast I found him pale and harassed, his bright eyes the brighter for the dark shadows round them. The carpet round his chair was littered with cigarette ends and with the early editions of the morning papers. An open telegram lay upon the table.

"What do you think of this, Watson?" he asked, tossing it across.

It was from Norwood, and ran as follows:

> Important fresh evidence to hand. McFarlane's guilt definitely established. Advise you to abandon case.
>
> LESTRADE.

"This sounds serious," said I.

"It is Lestrade's little cock-a-doodle of victory," Holmes answered, with a bitter smile. "And yet it may be premature to abandon the case. After all, important fresh evidence is a two-edged thing, and may possibly cut in a very different direction to that which Lestrade imagines. Take your breakfast, Watson, and we will go out together and see what we can do. I feel as if I shall need your company and your moral support today."

My friend had no breakfast himself, for it was one of his peculiarities that in his more intense moments he would permit himself no food, and I have known him to presume upon his iron strength until he has fainted from pure inanition. "At present I cannot spare energy and nerve force for digestion," he would say in answer to my medical remonstrances. I was not surprised, therefore, when this morning he left his untouched meal behind him, and started with me for Norwood. A crowd of morbid sightseers were still gathered round Deep Dene House, which was just such a suburban villa as I had pictured. Within the gates Lestrade met us, his face flushed with victory, his manner grossly triumphant.

"Well, Mr. Holmes, have you proved us to be wrong yet? Have you found your tramp?" he cried.

"I have formed no conclusion whatever," my companion answered.

"But we formed ours yesterday, and now it proves to be correct, so you must acknowledge that we have been a little in front of you this time, Mr. Holmes."

"You certainly have the air of something unusual having occurred," said Holmes.

Lestrade laughed loudly.

"You don't like being beaten any more than the rest of us do," said he. "A man can't expect always to have it his own way, can he, Dr. Watson? Step this way, if you please, gentlemen, and I think I can convince you once for all that it was John McFarlane who did this crime."

He led us through the passage and out into a dark hall beyond.

"This is where young McFarlane must have come out to get his hat after the crime was done," said he. "Now look at this." With dramatic suddenness he struck a match, and by its light exposed the stain of blood upon the whitewashed wall. As he held the match nearer, I saw that it was more than a stain. It was the well-marked print of a thumb.

"Look at that with your magnifying glass, Mr. Holmes."

"Yes, I am doing so."

"You are aware that no two thumb-marks are alike?"

"I have heard something of the kind."

"Well, then, will you please compare that print with this wax impression of young McFarlane's right thumb, taken by my orders this morning?"

As he held the waxen print close to the blood-stain, it did not take a magnifying glass to see that the two were undoubtedly from the same thumb. It was evident to me that our unfortunate client was lost.

"That is final," said Lestrade.

"Yes, that is final," I involuntarily echoed.

"It is final," said Holmes.

Something in his tone caught my ear, and I turned to look at him. An extraordinary change had come over his face. It was writhing with inward merriment. His two eyes were shining like stars. It seemed to me that he was making desperate efforts to restrain a convulsive attack of laughter.

"Dear me! Dear me!" he said at last. "Well, now, who would have thought it? And how deceptive appearances may be, to be sure! Such a nice young man to look at! It is a lesson to us not to trust our own judgment, is it not, Lestrade?"

"Yes, some of us are a little too much inclined to be cock-sure, Mr. Holmes," said Lestrade. The man's insolence was maddening, but we could not resent it.

"What a providential thing that this young man should press his right thumb against the wall in taking his hat from the peg! Such a very natural action, too, if you come to think of it." Holmes was outwardly calm, but his whole body gave a wriggle of suppressed excitement as he spoke.

"By the way, Lestrade, who made this remarkable discovery?"

"It was the housekeeper, Mrs. Lexington, who drew the night constable's attention to it."

"Where was the night constable?"

"He remained on guard in the bedroom where the crime was committed, so as to see that nothing was touched."

"But why didn't the police see this mark yesterday?"

"Well, we had no particular reason to make a careful examination of the hall. Besides, it's not a very prominent place, as you see."

"No, no—of course not. I suppose there is no doubt that the mark was there yesterday?"

Lestrade looked at Holmes as if he thought he was going out of his mind. I confess that I was myself surprised both at his hilarious manner and at his rather wild observation.

"I don't know whether you think that McFarlane came out of jail in the dead of the night in order to strengthen the evidence against himself," said Lestrade. "I leave it to any expert in the world whether that is not the mark of his thumb."

"It is unquestionably the mark of his thumb."

"There, that's enough," said Lestrade. "I am a practical man, Mr. Holmes, and when I have got my evidence I come to my conclusions. If you have anything to say, you will find me writing my report in the sitting room."

Holmes had recovered his equanimity, though I still seemed to detect gleams of amusement in his expression.

"Dear me, this is a very sad development, Watson, is it not?" said he. "And yet there are singular points about it which hold out some hopes for our client."

"I am delighted to hear it," said I, heartily. "I was afraid it was all up with him."

"I would hardly go so far as to say that, my dear Watson. The fact is that there is one really serious flaw in this evidence to which our friend attaches so much importance."

"Indeed, Holmes! What is it?"

"Only this: That I *know* that that mark was not there when I examined the hall yesterday. And now, Watson, let us have a little stroll round in the sunshine.

With a confused brain, but with a heart into which some warmth of hope was returning, I accompanied my friend in a walk round the garden. Holmes took each face of the house in turn, and examined it with great interest. He then led the way inside, and went over the whole building from basement to attic. Most of the rooms were unfurnished, but none the less Holmes inspected them all minutely. Finally, on the top corridor, which ran outside three untenanted bedrooms, he again was seized with a spasm of merriment.

"There are really some very unique features about this case, Watson," said he. "I think it is time now that we took our friend Lestrade into our confidence. He has had his little smile at our expense, and perhaps we may do as much by him, if my reading of this problem proves to be correct. Yes, yes, I think I see how we should approach it."

The Scotland Yard inspector was still writing in the parlor when Holmes interrupted him.

"I understood that you were writing a report of this case," said he.

"So I am."

"Don't you think it may be a little premature? I can't help thinking that your evidence is not complete."

Lestrade knew my friend too well to disregard his words. He laid down his pen and looked curiously at him.

"What do you mean, Mr. Holmes?"

"Only that there is an important witness whom you have not seen."

"Can you produce him?"

"I think I can."

"Then do so."

"I will do my best. How many constables have you?"

"There are three within call."

"Excellent!" said Holmes. "May I ask if they are all large, able-bodied men with powerful voices?"

"I have no doubt they are, though I fail to see what their voices have to do with it."

"Perhaps I can help you to see that and one or two other things as well," said Holmes. "Kindly summon your men, and I will try."

Five minutes later, three policemen had assembled in the hall.

"In the outhouse you will find a considerable quantity of straw," said Holmes. "I will ask you to carry in two bundles of it. I think it will be of the greatest assistance in producing the witness whom I require. Thank you very much. I believe you have some matches in your pocket, Watson. Now, Mr. Lestrade, I will ask you all to accompany me to the top landing."

As I have said, there was a broad corridor there, which ran outside three empty bedrooms. At one end of the corridor we were all marshaled by Sherlock Holmes, the constables grinning and Lestrade staring at my friend with amazement, expectation, and derision chasing each other across his features. Holmes stood before us with the air of a conjurer who is performing a trick.

"Would you kindly send one of your constables for two buckets of water? Put the straw on the floor here, free from the wall on either side. Now I think that we are all ready."

Lestrade's face had begun to grow red and angry.

"I don't know whether you are playing a game with us, Mr. Sherlock Holmes," said he. "If you know anything you can surely say it without all this tomfoolery."

"I assure you, my good Lestrade, that I have an excellent reason for everything that I do. You may possibly remember that you chaffed me a little, some hours ago, when the sun seemed on your side of the hedge, so you must not grudge me a little pomp and ceremony now. Might I ask you, Watson, to open that window, and then to put a match to the edge of the straw?"

I did so, and driven by the draught, a coil of gray smoke swirled down the corridor, while the dry straw crackled and flamed.

"Now we must see if we can find this witness for you, Lestrade. Might I ask you all to join in the cry of 'Fire!'? Now then; one, two, three—"

"Fire!" we all yelled.

"Thank you. I will trouble you once again."

"Fire!"

"Just once more, gentlemen, and all together."

"Fire!" The shout must have rung over Norwood.

It had hardly died away when an amazing thing happened. A door suddenly flew open out of what appeared to be a solid wall at the end of the corridor, and a little, wizened man darted out of it, like a rabbit out of its burrow.

"Capital!" said Holmes, calmly. "Watson, a bucket of water over the straw. That will do! Lestrade, allow me to present you with your principal missing witness, Mr. Jonas Oldacre."

The detective stared at the newcomer with blank amazement. The latter was blinking in the bright light of the corridor, and peering at us and at the smoldering fire. It was an odious face—crafty, vicious, malignant, with shifty, light gray eyes and white lashes.

"What's this, then?" said Lestrade, at last. 'What have you been doing all this time, eh?"

Oldacre gave an uneasy laugh, shrinking back from the furious red face of the angry detective.

"I have done no harm."

"No harm? You have done your best to get an innocent man hanged. If it wasn't for this gentleman here, I am not sure that you would not have succeeded."

The wretched creature began to whimper.

"I am sure, sir, it was only my practical joke."

"Oh! A joke, was it? You won't find the laugh on your side, I promise you. Take him down, and keep him in the sitting room until I come. Mr. Holmes," he continued, when they had gone, "I could not speak before the constables, but I don't mind saying, in the presence of Dr. Watson, that this is the brightest thing that you have done yet, though it is a mystery to me how you did it. You have saved an innocent man's life, and you have prevented a very grave scandal, which would have ruined my reputation in the Force."

Holmes smiled, and clapped Lestrade upon the shoulder.

"Instead of being ruined, my good sir, you will find that your reputation has been enormously enhanced. Just make a few alterations in that report which you were writing, and they will understand how hard it is to throw dust in the eyes of Inspector Lestrade."

"And you don't want your name to appear?"

"Not at all. The work is its own reward. Perhaps I shall get the credit also at some distant day, when I permit my zealous historian to lay out his foolscap once more—eh, Watson? Well, now, let us see where this rat has been lurking."

A lath-and-plaster partition had been run across the passage six feet from the end, with a door cunningly concealed in it. It was lit within by slits under the eaves. A few articles of furniture and a supply of food and water were within, together with a number of books and papers.

"There's the advantage of being a builder," said Holmes, as we came out. "He was able to fix up his own little hiding place without any confederate—save, of course, that precious housekeeper of his, whom I should lose no time in adding to your bag, Lestrade."

"I'll take your advice. But how did you know of this place, Mr. Holmes?"

"I made up my mind that the fellow was hiding in the house. When I paced one corridor and found it six feet shorter than the corresponding one below, it was pretty clear where he was. I thought he had not the nerve to lie quiet before an alarm of fire. We could, of course, have gone in and taken him, but it amused me to make him reveal himself. Besides, I owed you a little mystification, Lestrade, for your chaff in the morning."

"Well, sir, you certainly got equal with me on that. But how in the world did you know that he was in the house at all?"

"The thumb mark, Lestrade. You said it was final; and so it was, in a very different sense. I knew it had not been there the day before. I pay a good deal of attention to matters of detail, as you may have observed, and I had examined the hall, and was sure that the wall was clear. Therefore, it had been put on during the night."

"But how?"

"Very simply. When those packets were sealed up, Jonas Oldacre got McFarlane to secure one of the seals by putting his thumb upon the soft wax. It would be done so quickly and so naturally, that I daresay the young man himself has no recollection of it. Very likely it just so happened, and Oldacre had himself no notion of the use he would put it to. Brooding over the case in that den of his, it suddenly struck him what absolutely damning evidence he could make against McFarlane by using that thumb mark. It was the simplest thing in the world for him to take a wax impression from the seal, to moisten it in as much blood as he could get from a pinprick, and to put the mark upon the wall during the night, either with his own hand or with that of his housekeeper. If you examine among those documents which he took with him into his retreat, I will lay you a wager that you find the seal with the thumb mark upon it."

"Wonderful!" said Lestrade. "Wonderful! It's all as clear as crystal, as you put it. But what is the object of this deep deception, Mr. Holmes?"

It was amusing to me to see how the detective's overbearing manner had changed suddenly to that of a child asking questions of its teacher.

"Well, I don't think that is very hard to explain. A very deep, malicious, vindictive person is the gentleman who is now awaiting us downstairs. You know that he was once refused by McFarlane's mother? You don't! I told you that you should go to Blackheath first and Norwood afterwards. Well, this injury, as he would consider it, has rankled in his wicked, scheming brain, and all his life he has longed for vengeance, but never seen his chance. During the last year or two, things have gone against him—secret speculation, I think—and he finds himself in a bad way. He determined to swindle his creditors, and for this purpose he pays large checks to a certain Mr. Cornelius, who is, I imagine, himself under another name. I have not traced these checks yet, but I have no doubt that they were banked under that name at some provincial town where Oldacre from time to time led a double existence. He intended to change his name altogether, draw this money, and vanish, starting life again elsewhere."

"Well, that's likely enough."

"It would strike him that in disappearing he might throw all pursuit off his track, and at the same time have an ample and crushing revenge upon his old sweetheart, if he could give the impression that he had been murdered by her only child. It was a masterpiece of villainy, and he carried it out like a master. The idea of the will, which would give an obvious motive for the crime, the secret visit unknown to his own parents, the retention of the stick, the blood, and the animal remains and buttons in the woodpile, all were admirable. It was a net from which it seemed to me, a few hours ago, that there was no possible escape. But he had not that supreme gift of the artist, the knowledge of when to stop. He wished to improve that which was already perfect—to draw the rope tighter yet round the neck of his unfortunate victim—and so he ruined all. Let us descend, Lestrade. There are just one or two questions that I would ask him."

The malignant creature was seated in his own parlor with a policeman upon each side of him.

"It was a joke, my good sir—a practical joke, nothing more," he whined incessantly. "I assure you, sir, that I simply concealed myself in order to see the effect of my disappearance, and I am sure that you would not be so unjust as to imagine that I would have allowed any harm to befall poor young Mr. McFarlane."

"That's for a jury to decide," said Lestrade. "Anyhow, we shall have you on a charge of conspiracy, if not for attempted murder."

"And you'll probably find that your creditors will impound the banking account of Mr. Cornelius," said Holmes.

The little man started, and turned his malignant eyes upon my friend.

"I have to thank you for a good deal," said he. "Perhaps I'll pay my debt some day."

Holmes smiled indulgently.

"I fancy that, for some few years, you will find your time very fully occupied," said he. "By the way, what was it you put into the woodpile besides your old trousers? A dead dog, or rabbits, or what? You won't tell? Dear me, how very unkind of you! Well, well, I daresay that a couple of rabbits would account both for the blood and for the charred ashes. If ever you write an account, Watson, you can make rabbits serve your turn."

Ambrose Bierce

Beyond the Wall

Many years ago, on my way from Hong Kong to New York, I passed a week in San Francisco. A long time had gone by since I had been in that city, during which my ventures in the Orient had prospered beyond my hope; I was rich and could afford to revisit my own country to renew my friendship with such of the companions of my youth as still lived and remembered me with the old affection. Chief of these, I hoped, was Mohun Dampier, an old schoolmate with whom I had held a desultory correspondence which had long ceased, as is the way of correspondence between men. You may have observed that the indisposition to write a merely social letter is in the ratio of the square of the distance between you and your correspondent. It is a law.

I remembered Dampier as a handsome, strong young fellow of scholarly tastes, with an aversion to work and a marked indifference to many of the things that the world cares for, including wealth, of which, however, he had inherited enough to put him beyond the reach of want. In this family, one of the oldest and most aristocratic in the country, it was, I think, a matter of pride that no member of it had ever been in trade nor politics, nor suffered any kind of distinction. Mohun was a trifle sentimental, and had in him a singular element of superstition, which led him to the study of all manner of occult subjects, although his sane mental health safeguarded him against fantastic and perilous faiths. He made daring incursions into the realm of the unreal without renouncing his residence in the partly surveyed and charted region of what we are pleased to call certitude.

The night of my visit to him was stormy. The California winter was on, and the incessant rain splashed in the deserted streets, or, lifted by irregular gusts of wind, was hurled against the houses with incredible fury. With no small difficulty my cabman found the right place, away out toward the ocean beach, in a sparsely populated suburb. The dwelling, a rather ugly one, apparently, stood in the center of its grounds, which as nearly as I could make out in the gloom were destitute of either flowers or grass. Three or four trees, writhing and moaning in the torment of the tempest, appeared to be trying to escape from their dismal environment and take the chance of finding a better one out at sea. The house was a two-story brick structure with a tower, a story higher, at one corner. In a window of that was the only visible light. Something in the appearance of the place made me shudder, a performance that may have been assisted by a rill of rainwater down my back as I scuttled to cover in the doorway.

In answer to my note apprising him of my wish to call, Dampier had written, "Don't ring—open the door and come up." I did so. The staircase was dimly lighted by a single gas jet at the top of the second flight. I managed to reach the landing without disaster and entered by an open door into the lighted square room of the tower. Dampier came forward in gown and slippers to receive me, giving me the greeting that I wished, and if I had held a thought that it might more fitly have been accorded me at the front door the first look at him dispelled any sense of his inhospitality.

He was not the same. Hardly past middle age, he had gone gray and acquired a pronounced stoop. His figure was thin and angular, his face deeply lined, his complexion dead white, without a touch of color. His eyes, unnaturally large, glowed with a fire that was almost uncanny.

He seated me, proffered a cigar, and with grave and obvious sincerity assured me of the pleasure that it gave him to meet me. Some unimportant conversation followed, but all the while I was dominated by a melancholy sense of the great change in him. This he must have perceived, for he suddenly said with a bright enough smile, "You are disappointed in me—*non sum qualis eram.*"

I hardly knew what to reply, but managed to say: "Why, really, I don't know; your Latin is about the same."

He brightened again. "No," he said, "being a dead language, it grows in appropriateness. But please have the patience to wait; where I am going there is perhaps a better tongue. Will you care to have a message in it?"

The smile faded as he spoke, and as he concluded he was looking into my eyes with a gravity that distressed me. Yet I would not surrender myself to his mood, nor permit him to see how deeply his prescience of death affected me.

"I fancy that it will be long," I said, "before human speech will cease to serve our need; and then the need, with its possibilities of service, will have passed."

He made no reply, and I too was silent, for the talk had taken a dispiriting turn, yet I knew not how to give it a more agreeable character. Suddenly, in a pause of the storm, when the dead silence was almost startling by contrast with the previous uproar, I heard a gentle tapping, which appeared to come from the wall behind my chair. The sound was such as might have been made by a human hand, not as upon a door by one asking admittance, but rather, I thought, as an agreed signal, an assurance of someone's presence in an adjoining room; most of us, I fancy, have had more experience of such communications than we should care to relate. I glanced at Dampier. If possibly there was something of amusement in the look he did not observe it. He appeared to have forgotten my presence, and was staring at the wall behind me with an expression in his eyes that I am unable to name, although my memory of it is as vivid today as was my sense of it then. The situation was embarrassing; I rose to take my leave. At this he seemed to recover himself.

"Please be seated," he said; "it is nothing—no one is there."

But the tapping was repeated, and with the same gentle, slow insistence as before.

"Pardon me," I said, "it is late. May I call tomorrow?"

He smiled—a little mechanically, I thought. "It is very delicate of you," he said, "but quite needless. Really, this is the only room in the tower, and no one is there. At least—" He left the sentence incomplete, rose, and threw up a window, the only opening in the wall from which the sound seemed to come. "See."

Not clearly knowing what else to do I followed him to the window and looked out. A streetlamp some little distance away gave enough light through the murk of the rain that was again falling in torrents to make it entirely plain that "no one was there." In truth there was nothing but the sheer blank wall of the tower.

Dampier closed the window and, signing me to my seat, resumed his own.

The incident was not in itself particularly mysterious; any one of a dozen explanations was possible (though none has occurred to me), yet it impressed me strangely, the more, perhaps, from my friend's effort to reassure me, which seemed to dignify it with a certain significance and importance. He had proved that no one was there, but in that fact lay all the interest; and he proffered no explanation. His silence was irritating and made me resentful.

"My good friend," I said, somewhat ironically, I fear, "I am not disposed to question your right to harbor as many spooks as you find agreeable to your taste and consistent with your notions of companionship; that is no business of mine. But being just a plain man of affairs, mostly of this world, I find spooks needless to my peace and comfort. I am going to my hotel, where my fellow guests are still in the flesh."

It was not a very civil speech, but he manifested no feeling about it. "Kindly remain," he said. "I am grateful for your presence here. What you have heard, tonight I believe myself to have heard twice before. Now I *know* it was no illusion. That is much to me—more than you know. Have a fresh cigar and a good stock of patience while I tell you the story."

The rain was now falling more steadily, with a low, monotonous susurration, interrupted at long intervals by the sudden slashing of the boughs of the trees as the wind rose and failed. The night was well advanced, but both sympathy and curiosity held me a willing listener to my friend's monologue, which I did not interrupt by a single word from beginning to end.

"Ten years ago," he said, "I occupied a ground-floor apartment in one of a row of houses, all alike, away at the other end of the town, on what we call Rincon Hill. This had been the best quarter of San Francisco, but had fallen into neglect and decay, partly because the primitive character of its domestic architecture no longer suited the maturing tastes of our wealthy citizens, partly because certain public improvements had made a wreck of it. The row of dwellings in one of which I lived stood a little way back from the street, each having a miniature garden, separated from its neighbors by low iron fences and bisected with mathematical precision by a box-bordered gravel walk from gate to door.

"One morning as I was leaving my lodging I

observed a young girl entering the adjoining garden on the left. It was a warm day in June, and she was lightly gowned in white. From her shoulders hung a broad straw hat profusely decorated with flowers and wonderfully beribboned in the fashion of the time. My attention was not long held by the exquisite simplicity of her costume, for no one could look at her face and think of anything earthly. Do not fear; I shall not profane it by description; it was beautiful exceedingly. All that I had ever seen or dreamed of loveliness was in that matchless living picture by the hand of the Divine Artist. So deeply did it move me that, without a thought of the impropriety of the act, I unconsciously bared my head, as a devout Catholic or well-bred Protestant uncovers before an image of the Blessed Virgin. The maiden showed no displeasure; she merely turned her glorious dark eyes upon me with a look that made me catch my breath, and without other recognition of my act passed into the house. For a moment I stood motionless, hat in hand, painfully conscious of my rudeness, yet so dominated by the emotion inspired by that vision of incomparable beauty that my penitence was less poignant than it should have been. Then I went my way, leaving my heart behind. In the natural course of things I should probably have remained away until nightfall, but by the middle of the afternoon I was back in the little garden, affecting an interest in the few foolish flowers that I had never before observed. My hope was vain; she did not appear.

"To a night of unrest succeeded a day of expectation and disappointment, but on the day after, as I wandered aimlessly about the neighborhood, I met her. Of course I did not repeat my folly of uncovering, nor venture by even so much as too long a look to manifest an interest in her; yet my heart was beating audibly. I trembled and consciously colored as she turned her big black eyes upon me with a look of obvious recognition entirely devoid of boldness or coquetry.

"I will not weary you with particulars; many times afterward I met the maiden, yet never either addressed her or sought to fix her attention. Nor did I take any action toward making her acquaintance. Perhaps my forbearance, requiring so supreme an effort of self-denial, will not be entirely clear to you. That I was heels over head in love is true, but who can overcome his habit of thought, or reconstruct his character?

"I was what some foolish persons are pleased to call, and others, more foolish, are pleased to be called—an aristocrat; and despite her beauty, her charms and graces, the girl was not of my class. I had learned her name—which it is needless to speak—and something of her family. She was an orphan, a dependent niece of the impossible elderly fat woman in whose lodging house she lived. My income was small and I lacked the talent for marrying; it is perhaps a gift. An alliance with that family would condemn me to its manner of life, part me from my books and studies, and in a social sense reduce me to the ranks. It is easy to deprecate such considerations of these and I have not retained myself for the defense. Let judgment be entered against me, but in strict justice all my ancestors for generations should be made co-defendants and

I be permitted to plead in mitigation of punishment the imperious mandate of heredity. To a mesalliance of that kind every globule of my ancestral blood spoke in opposition. In brief, my tastes, habits, instinct, with whatever of reason my love had left me—all fought against it. Moreover, I was an irreclaimable sentimentalist, and found a subtle charm in an impersonal and spiritual relation which acquaintance might vulgarize and marriage would certainly dispel. No woman, I argued, is what this lovely creature seems. Love is a delicious dream; why should I bring about my own awakening?

"The course dictated by all this sense and sentiment was obvious. Honor, pride, prudence, preservation of my ideals—all commanded me to go away, but for that I was too weak. The utmost that I could do by a mighty effort of will was to cease meeting the girl, and that I did. I even avoided the chance encounters of the garden, leaving my lodging only when I knew that she had gone to her music lessons, and returning after nightfall. Yet all the while I was as one in a trance, indulging the most fascinating fancies and ordering my entire intellectual life in accordance with my dream. Ah, my friend, as one whose actions have a traceable relation to reason, you cannot know the fool's paradise in which I lived.

"One evening the devil put it into my head to be an unspeakable idiot. By apparently careless and purposeless questioning I learned from my gossipy landlady that the young woman's bedroom ajoined my own, a party wall between. Yielding to a sudden and coarse impulse I gently rapped on the wall. There was no response, naturally, but

I was in no mood to accept a rebuke. A madness was upon me and I repeated the folly, the offense, but again ineffectually, and I had the decency to desist.

"An hour later, while I absorbed in some of my infernal studies, I heard, or thought I heard, my signal answered. Flinging down my books I sprang to the wall and as steadily as my beating heart would permit gave three slow taps upon it. This time the response was distinct, unmistakable: one, two, three—an exact repetition of my signal. That was all I could elicit, but it was enough—too much.

"The next evening, and for many evenings afterward, that folly went on, I always having 'the last word.' During the whole period I was deliriously happy, but with the perversity of my nature I persevered in my resolution not to see her. Then, as I should have expected, I got no further answers. 'She is disgusted,' I said to myself, 'with what she thinks my timidity in making no more definite advances'; and I resolved to seek her and make her acquaintance and—what? I did not know, nor do I now know, what might have come of it. I know only that I passed days and days trying to meet her, and all in vain; she was invisible as well as inaudible. I haunted the streets where we had met, but she did not come. From my window I watched the garden in front of her house, but she passed neither in nor out. I fell into the deepest dejection, believing that she had gone away, yet took no steps to resolve my doubt by inquiry of my landlady, to whom, indeed, I had taken an unconquerable aversion from her having once spoken of the girl with less of reverence than I thought befitting.

"There came a fateful night. Worn out with emotion, irresolution and despondency, I had retired early and fallen into such sleep as was still possible to me. In the middle of the night something—some malign power bent upon the wrecking of my peace forever—caused me to open my eyes and sit up, wide awake and listening intently for I knew not what. Then I thought I heard a faint tapping on the wall—the mere ghost of the familiar signal. In a few moments it was repeated: one, two, three—no louder than before, but addressing a sense alert and strained to receive it. I was about to reply when the Adversary of Peace again intervened in my affairs with a rascally suggestion of retaliation. She had long and cruelly ignored me; now I would ignore her. Incredible fatuity—may God forgive it! All the rest of the night I lay awake, fortifying my obstinacy with shameless justification and—listening.

"Late the next morning, as I was leaving the house, I met my landlady, entering.

" 'Good morning, Mr. Dampier,' she said. 'Have you heard the news?'

"I replied in words that I had heard no news; in manner, that I did not care to hear any. The manner escaped her observation.

" 'About the sick young lady next door,' she babbled on. 'What! You did not know? Why, she has been ill for weeks. And now—'

"I almost sprang upon her. 'And now,' I cried, 'now what?'

" 'She is dead.'

"That is not the whole story. In the middle of the night, as I learned later, the patient, awakening from a long stupor after a week of delirium, had asked—it was her last utterance—that her bed be moved to the opposite side of the room. Those in attendance had thought the request a vagary of her delirium, but had complied. And there the poor passing soul had exerted its failing will to restore a broken connection—a golden thread of sentiment between its innocence and a monstrous baseness owning a blind, brutal allegiance to the Law of Self.

"What reparation could I make? Are there masses that can be said for the repose of souls that are abroad such nights as this—spirits 'blown about by the viewless winds'—coming in the storm and darkness with signs and portents, hints of memory and presages of doom?

"This is the third visitation. On the first occasion I was too skeptical to do more than verify by natural methods the character of the incident; on the second, I responded to the signal after it had been several times repeated, but without result. Tonight's recurrence completes the 'fatal triad' expounded by Parapelius Necromantius. There is no more to tell."

When Dampier had finished his story I could think of nothing relevant that I cared to say, and to question him would have been a hideous impertinence. I rose and bade him good night in a way to convey to him a sense of my sympathy, which he silently acknowledged by a pressure of the hand. That night, alone with his sorrow and remorse, he passed into the Unknown.

Washington Irving

The Specter Bridegroom

On the summit of one of the heights of the Odenwald, a wild and romantic tract of Upper Germany that lies not far from the confluence of the Main and the Rhine, there stood, many, many years since, the Castle of the Baron Von Landshort. It is now quite fallen to decay and almost buried among beech trees and dark firs, above which, however, its old watchtower may still be seen, struggling, like the former possessor I have mentioned, to carry a high head and look down upon the neighboring country.

The baron was a dry branch of the great family of Katzenellenbogen, and inherited the relics of the property and all the pride of his ancestors. Though the warlike disposition of his predecessors had much impaired the family possessions, yet the baron still endeavored to keep up some show of former state. The times were peaceable, and the German nobles, in general, had abandoned their inconvenient old castles, perched like eagles' nests among the mountains, and had built more convenient residences in the valleys; still the baron remained proudly drawn up in his little fortress, cherishing, with hereditary inveteracy, all the old family feuds, so that he was on ill terms with some of his nearest neighbors on account of disputes that had happened between their great-great-grandfathers.

The baron had but one child, a daughter; but nature, when she grants but one child, always compensates by making it a prodigy, and so it was with the daughter of the baron. All the nurses, gossips, and country cousins assured her father that she had not her equal for beauty in all Germany; and who should know better than they? She had, moreover, been brought up with great care under the superintendence of two maiden aunts, who had spent some years of their early life at one of the little German courts and were skilled in all the branches of knowledge necessary to the education of a fine lady. Under their instructions she became a miracle of accomplishments. By the time she was eighteen she could embroider to admiration and had worked whole histories of the saints in tapestry with such strength of expression in their countenances that they looked like so many souls in purgatory. She could read without great difficulty, and had spelled her way through several church legends and almost all the chivalric wonders of the Heldenbuch. She had even made considerable proficiency in writing, could sign her own name without missing a letter, and so legibly that her aunts could read it without spectacles. She excelled in making little elegant good-for-nothing ladylike knickknacks of all kinds; was versed in the most abstruse dancing of the day; played a number of airs on the harp and guitar; and knew all the tender ballads of the Minnelieders by heart.

Her aunts, too, having been great flirts and coquettes in their younger days, were admirably calculated to be vigilant guardians and strict censors of the conduct of their niece, for there is no duenna so rigidly prudent and inexorably decorous as a superannuated coquette. She was rarely suffered out of their sight; never went beyond the domains of the castle, unless well attended, or rather well watched; had continual lectures read to her about strict decorum and implicit obedience; and, as to the men—pah! She was taught to hold them at such a distance, and in such absolute distrust, that, unless properly authorized, she would not have cast a glance upon the handsomest cavalier in the world—no, not if he were even dying at her feet.

The good effects of this system were wonderfully apparent. The young lady was a pattern of docility and correctness. While others were wasting their sweetness in the glare of the world and liable to be plucked and thrown aside by every hand, she was coyly blooming into fresh and lovely womanhood under the protection of those immaculate spinsters, like a rosebud blushing forth among guardian thorns. Her aunts looked upon her with pride and exultation, and vaunted that though all the other young ladies in the world might go astray, yet, thank Heaven, nothing of the kind could happen to the heiress of Katzenellenbogen.

But, however scantily the Baron Von Landshort might be provided with children, his household was by no means a small one, for Providence had enriched him with abundance of poor relations. They, one and all, possessed the affectionate disposition common to humble relatives, were wonderfully attached to the baron, and took every possible occasion to come in swarms and enliven the castle. All family festivals were commemorated by these good people at the baron's expense; and when they were filled with good cheer they would declare that there was nothing on earth so delightful as these family meetings, these jubilees of the heart.

The baron, though a small man, had a large soul, and it swelled with satisfaction at the consciousness of being the greatest man in the little world about him. He loved to tell long stories about the dark old warriors whose portraits looked grimly down from the walls around, and he found no listeners equal to those that fed at his expense. He was much given to the marvelous, and a firm believer in all those supernatural tales with which every mountain and valley in Germany abounds. The faith of his guests exceeded even his own; they listened to every tale of wonder with open eyes and mouth, and never failed to be astonished, even though repeated for the hundredth time. Thus lived the Baron Von Landshort, the oracle of his table, the absolute monarch of his little territory, and happy, above all things, in the persuasion that he was the wisest man of his age.

At the time of which my story treats there was a great family gathering at the castle, on an affair of the utmost importance; it was to receive the destined bridegroom of the baron's daughter. A negotiation had been carried on between the father and an old nobleman of Bavaria to unite the dignity of their houses by the marriage of their children. The preliminaries had been conducted with proper punctilio. The young people were betrothed without seeing each other, and the time was appointed for the marriage ceremony. The young Count Von Altenburg had been recalled from the army for the purpose, and was actually on his way to the baron's to receive his bride. Missives had even been received from him, from Würzburg, where he had accidentally detained, mentioning the day and hour when he might be expected to arrive.

The castle was in a tumult of preparation to give him a suitable welcome. The fair bride had been decked out with uncommon care. The two aunts had superintended her toilet and quarreled the whole morning about every article of her dress. The young lady had taken advantage of their contest to follow the bent of her own taste, and fortunately it was a good one. She looked as lovely as youthful bridegroom could desire, and the flutter of expectation heightened the luster of her charms.

The suffusions that mantled her face and neck, the gentle sighs, the eye now and then lost in reverie, all betrayed the soft tumult that was going on in her little heart. The aunts were continually hovering around her, for maiden aunts are apt to take great interest in affairs of this nature. They were giving her a world of staid counsel how to deport herself, what to say, and in what manner to receive the expected lover.

The baron was no less busied in preparations. He had, in truth, nothing exactly to do, but he was naturally a fuming bustling little man, and could not remain passive when all the world was in a hurry. He worried from top to bottom of the castle with an air of infinite anxiety; he continually called the servants from their work to exhort them to be diligent; and buzzed about every hall and chamber, as idly restless and importunate as a bluebottle fly on a warm summer's day.

In the meantime the fatted calf had been killed; the forests had rung with the clamor of the huntsmen; the kitchen was crowded with good cheer; the cellars had yielded up whole oceans of *Rhein-wein* and *Ferne-wein;* and even the great Heidelberg vat had been laid under contribution. Everything was ready to receive the distinguished guest with *Saus und Braus* in the true spirit of German hospitality—but the guest delayed to make his appearance. Hour rolled after hour. The sun that had poured his downward rays upon the rich forest of the Odenwald now just gleamed along the summits of the mountains. The baron mounted the highest tower, and strained his eyes in hope of catching a distant sight of the count and his attendants. Once he thought he beheld them; the sound of horns came floating from the valley, prolonged by the mountain echoes. A number of horsemen were seen far below, slowly advancing along the road; but when they had nearly reached the foot of the mountains they suddenly struck off in a different direction. The last ray of sunshine departed—the bats began to flit by in the twilight—the road grew dimmer and dimmer to the view; and nothing appeared stirring in it but now and then a peasant lagging homeward from his labor.

While the old castle of Landshort was in this state of perplexity a very interesting scene was transacting in a different part of the Odenwald.

The young Count Von Altenburg was tranquilly pursuing his route in that sober jog-trot way, in which a man travels toward matrimony when his friends have taken all the trouble and uncertainty of courtship off his hands, and a bride is waiting for him as certainly as a dinner at the end of his journey. He had encountered at Würzburg a youthful companion in arms with whom he had seen some service on the frontiers, Herman Von Starkenfaust, one of the stoutest hands and worthiest hearts of German chivalry, who was now returning from the army. His father's castle was not far distant from the old fortress of Landshort, although an hereditary feud rendered the families hostile and strangers to each other.

In the warmhearted moment of recognition the young friends related all their past adventures and fortunes, and the count gave the whole history of his intended nuptials with a young lady whom he had never seen but of whose charms he had received the most enrapturing descriptions.

As the route of the friends lay in the same direction, they agreed to perform the rest of their journey together; and, that they might do it the more leisurely, set off from Würzburg at an early hour, the count having given directions for his retinue to follow and overtake him.

They beguiled their wayfaring with recollections of their military scenes and adventures; but the count was apt to be a little tedious, now and then, about the reputed charms of his bride, and the felicity that awaited him.

In this way they had entered among the mountains of the Odenwald, and were traversing one of its most lonely and thickly wooded passes. It is well known that the forests of Germany have always been as much infested by robbers as its castles by specters; and at this time the former were particularly numerous, from the hordes of disbanded soldiers wandering about the country. It will not appear extraordinary, therefore, that the cavaliers were attacked by a gang of these stragglers in the midst of the forest. They defended themselves with bravery, but were nearly overpowered, when the count's retinue arrived to their assistance. At sight of them the robbers fled, but not until the count had received a mortal wound. He was slowly and carefully conveyed back to the city of Würzburg, and a friar summoned from a neighboring convent, who was famous for his skill in administering to both soul and body; but half of his skill was superfluous; the moments of the unfortunate count were numbered.

With his dying breath he entreated his friend to repair instantly to the castle of Landshort and explain the fatal cause of his not keeping his appointment with his bride. Though not the most ardent of lovers, he was one of the most punctilious of men, and appeared earnestly solicitous that his mission should be speedily and courteously executed. "Unless this is done," he said, "I shall not sleep quietly in my grave!" He repeated these last words with peculiar solemnity. A request, at a moment so impressive, admitted no hesitation. Starkenfaust endeavored to soothe him to calmness, promised faithfully to execute his wish and gave him his hand in solemn pledge. The dying man pressed it in acknowledgment, but soon lapsed into delirium—raved about his bride—his engagements—his plighted word; ordered his horse that he might ride to the castle of Landshort; and expired in the fancied act of vaulting into the saddle.

Starkenfaust bestowed a sigh and a soldier's tear on the untimely fate of his comrade, and then pondered on the awkward mission he had undertaken. His heart was heavy and his head perplexed, for he was to present himself an unbidden guest among hostile people, and to damp their festivity with tidings fatal to their hopes. Still there were certain whisperings of curiosity in his bosom to see this far-famed beauty of Katzenellenbogen, so cautiously shut up from the world, for he was a passionate admirer of women, and there was a dash of eccentricity and enterprise in his character that made him fond of all singular adventure.

Previous to his departure he made all due arrangements with the holy fraternity of the convent for the funeral solemnities of his friend, who was to be buried in the cathedral of Würzburg, near some of his illustrious relatives; and the mourning retinue of the count took charge of his remains.

It is now high time that we should return to the ancient family of Katzenellenbogen, who were impatient for their guest, and still more for their dinner; and to the worthy little baron, whom we left airing himself on the watchtower.

Night closed in, but still no guest arrived. The baron descended from the tower in despair. The banquet, which had been delayed from hour to hour, could no longer be postponed. The meats were already overdone; the cook in an agony; and the whole household had the look of a garrison that had been reduced by famine. The baron was obliged reluctantly to give orders for the feast without the presence of the guest. All were seated at table, and just on the point of commencing when the sound of a horn from without the gate gave notice of the approach of a stranger. Another long blast filled the old courts of the castle with its echoes, and was answered by the warder from the walls The baron hastened to receive his future son-in-law.

The drawbridge had been let down, and the stranger was before the gate. He was a tall, gallant cavalier, mounted on a black steed. His countenance was pale, but he had a beaming, romantic eye, and an air of stately melancholy. The baron was a little mortified that he should have come in this simple, solitary style. His dignity for a moment was ruffled, and he felt disposed to consider it a want of proper respect for the important occasion and the important family with which he was to be connected. He pacified himself, however, with the conclusion that it must have been youthful impatience which had induced him thus to spur on sooner than his attendants.

"I am sorry," said the stranger, "to break in upon you thus unseasonably——"

Here the baron interrupted him with a world of compliments and greetings, for, to tell the truth, he prided himself upon his courtesy and eloquence. The stranger attempted, once or twice, to stem the torrent of words, but in vain, so he bowed his head and suffered it to flow on. By the time the baron had come to a pause, they had reached the inner court of the castle, and the stranger was again about to speak when he was once more interrupted by the appearance of the female part of the family, leading forth the shrinking and blushing bride. He gazed on her for a moment as one entranced; it seemed as if his whole soul beamed forth in the gaze, and rested upon that lovely form. One of the maiden aunts whispered something in her ear; she made an effort to speak; her moist blue eye was timidly raised, gave a shy glance of inquiry on the stranger, and was cast again to the ground. The words died away, but there was a sweet smile playing about her lips and a soft dimpling of the cheek that showed her glance had not been unsatisfactory. It was impossible for a girl of the fond age of eighteen, highly predisposed for love and matrimony, not to be pleased with so gallant a cavalier.

The late hour at which the guest had arrived left no time for parley. The baron was peremptory, and deferred all particular conversation until the morning, and led the way to the untasted banquet.

It was served up in the great hall of the castle. Around the walls hung the hard-favored portraits of the heroes of the house of Katzenellenbogen and the trophies which they gained in the field and the in the chase. Hacked armor, splintered jousting spears, and tattered banners were mingled with the spoils of sylvan warfare; the jaws of the wolf and the tusks of the boar grinned horribly among crossbows and battle axes, and a huge pair of antlers branched immediately over the head of the youthful bridegroom.

The cavalier took but little notice of the company

or the entertainment. He scarcely tasted the banquet, but seemed absorbed in admiration of his bride. He conversed in a low tone that could not be overheard—for the language of love is never loud; but where is the female ear so dull that it cannot catch the softest whisper of the lover? There was a mingled tenderness and gravity in his manner that appeared to have a powerful effect upon the young lady. Her color came and went as she listened with deep attention. Now and then she made some blushing reply, and when his eye was turned away, she would steal a sidelong glance at his romantic countenance and heave a gentle sigh of tender happiness. It was evident that the young couple were completely enamored. The aunts, who were deeply versed in the mysteries of the heart, declared that they had fallen in love with each other at first sight.

The feast went on merrily, or at least noisily, for the guests were all blessed with those keen appetites that attend upon light purses and mountain air. The baron told his best and longest stories, and never had he told them so well or with such great effect. If there was anything marvelous, his auditors were lost in astonishment; and if anything facetious, they were sure to laugh exactly in the right place. The baron, it is true, like most great men, was too dignified to utter any joke but a dull one; it was always enforced, however, by a bumper of excellent Hockheimer, and even a dull joke, at one's own table, served up with jolly old wine, is irresistible. Many good things were said by poorer and keener wits that would not bear repeating, except on similar occasions; many sly speeches whispered in ladies' ears that almost convulsed them with suppressed laughter; and a song or two roared out by a poor but merry and broad-faced cousin of the baron that absolutely made the maiden aunts hold up their fans.

Amidst all this revelry, the stranger guest maintained a most singular and unseasonable gravity. His countenance assumed a deeper cast of dejection as the evening advanced; and, strange as it may appear, even the baron's jokes seemed only to render him the more melancholy. At times he was lost in thought, and at times there was a perturbed and restless wandering of the eye that bespoke a mind but ill at ease. His conversations with the bride became more and more earnest and mysterious. Lowering clouds began to steal over the fair serenity of her brow, and tremors to run through her tender frame.

All this could not escape the notice of the company. Their gaiety was chilled by the unaccountable gloom of the bridegroom; their spirits were infected; whispers and glances were interchanged, accompanied by shrugs and dubious shakes of the head. The song and the laugh grew less and less frequent; there were dreary pauses in the conversation, which were at length succeeded by wild tales and supernatural legends. One dismal story produced another still more dismal, and the baron nearly frightened some of the ladies into hysterics with the history of the goblin horseman that carried away the fair Leonora; a dreadful story, which had since been put into excellent verse, and is read and believed by all the world.

The bridegroom listened to this tale with profound attention. He kept his eyes steadily fixed on the baron, and, as the story drew to a close, began gradually to rise from his seat, growing taller and taller, until, in the baron's entranced eye, he seemed almost to tower into a giant. The moment the tale was finished, he heaved a deep sigh, and took a solemn farewell of the company. They were all amazement. The baron was perfectly thunderstruck.

"What! Going to leave the castle at midnight? Why, everything was prepared for his reception; a chamber was ready for him if he wished to retire."

The stranger shook his head mournfully and mysteriously. "I must lay my head in a different chamber tonight!"

There was something in this reply and the tone in which it was uttered that made the baron's heart misgive him, but he rallied his forces and repeated his hospitable entreaties.

The stranger shook his head silently, but positively, at every offer; and, waving his farewell to the company, stalked slowly out of the hall. The maiden aunts were absolutely petrified—the bride hung her head, and a tear stole to her eye.

The baron followed the stranger to the great court of the castle, where the black charger stood pawing the earth, and snorting with impatience. When they had reached the portal, whose deep archway was dimly lighted by a cresset, the stranger paused, and addressed the baron in a hollow tone of voice, which the vaulted roof rendered still more sepulchral.

"Now that we are alone," said he, "I will impart to you the reason of my going. I have a solemn, an indispensable engagement——"

"Why," said the baron, "cannot you send someone in your place?"

"It admits of no substitute—I must attend it in person—I must away to Würzburg cathedral——"

"Ay," said the baron, plucking up spirit, "but not until tomorrow—tomorrow you shall take your bride there."

"No! No!" replied the stranger, with tenfold solemnity, "my engagement is with no bride—the worms! The worms expect me! I am a dead man—I have been slain by robbers—my body lies at Würzburg—at midnight I am to be buried—the grave is waiting for me—I must keep my appointment!"

He sprang on his black charger, dashed over the drawbridge, and the clattering of his horse's hoofs was lost in the whistling of the night blast.

The baron returned to the hall in the utmost consternation and related what had passed. The ladies fainted outright, others sickened at the idea of having banqueted with a specter. It was the opinion of some that this might be the wild huntsman, famous in German legend. Some talked of mountain sprites, of wood demons, and of other supernatural beings, with which the good people of Germany have been so grievously harassed since time immemorial. One of the poor relations ventured to suggest that it might be some sportive evasion of the young cavalier, and that the very gloominess of the caprice seemed to accord with so melancholy a personage. This, however, drew on him the indignation of the whole company, and especially of the baron, who looked upon him as little better than an infidel, so that he was fain to abjure his heresy as speedily as possible and come into the faith of the true believers.

But whatever may have been the doubts entertained, they were completely put to an end by the arrival, next day, of regular missives, confirming the intelligence of the young count's murder, and his interment in Würzburg cathedral.

The dismay at the castle may well be imagined. The baron shut himself up in his chamber. The guests, who had come to rejoice with him, could not think of abandoning him in his distress. They wandered about the courts, or collected in groups in the hall, shaking their heads and shrugging their shoulders at the troubles of so good a man; and sat longer than ever at table, and ate and drank more stoutly than ever, by way of keeping up their spirits. But the situation of the widowed bride was the most pitiable. To have lost a husband before she had even embraced him—and such a husband! If the very specter could be so gracious and noble, what must have been the living man? She filled the house with lamentations.

On the night of the second day of her widowhood, she had retired to her chamber, accompanied by one of her aunts, who insisted on sleeping with her. The aunt, who was one of the best tellers of ghost stories in all Germany, had just been recounting one of her longest, and had fallen asleep in the very midst of it. The chamber was remote, and overlooked a small garden. The niece lay pensively gazing at the beams of the rising moon, as they trembled on the leaves of an aspen tree before the lattice. The castle clock had just tolled midnight when a soft strain of music stole up from the garden. She rose hastily from her bed, and stepped lightly to the window. A tall figure stood among the shadows of the trees. As it raised its head, a beam of moonlight fell upon the countenance. Heaven and earth! She beheld the Specter Bridegroom! A loud shriek at that moment burst upon her ear, and her aunt, who had been awakened by the music and had followed her silently to the window, fell into her arms. When she looked again, the specter had disappeared.

Of the two females, the aunt now required the more soothing, for she was perfectly beside herself with terror. As to the young lady, there was something, even in the specter of her lover, that seemed endearing. There was still the semblance of manly beauty; and though the shadow of a man is but little calculated to satisfy the affections of a lovesick girl, yet, where the substance is not to be had, even that is consoling. The aunt declared she would never sleep in that chamber again; the niece, for once, was refractory, and declared as strongly that she would sleep in no other in the castle. The consequence was that she had to sleep in it alone; but she drew a promise from her aunt not to relate the story of the specter, lest she should be denied the only melancholy pleasure left her on earth—that of inhabiting the chamber over which the guardian shade of her lover kept its nightly vigils.

How long the good old lady would have observed this promise is uncertain, for she dearly loved to talk of the marvelous, and there is a triumph in being the first to tell a frightful story;

it is, however, still quoted in the neighborhood, as a memorable instance of female secrecy, that she kept it to herself for a whole week, when she was suddenly absolved from all further restraint by intelligence brought to the breakfast table one morning that the young lady was not to be found. Her room was empty—the bed had not been slept in—the window was open, and the bird had flown!

The astonishment and concern with which the intelligence was received can only be imagined by those who have witnessed the agitation which the mishaps of a great man cause among his friends. Even the poor relations paused for a moment from the indefatigable labors of the trencher, when the aunt, who had at first been struck speechless, wrung her hands, and shrieked out, "The goblin! The goblin! She's carried away by the goblin."

In a few words she related the fearful scene of the garden, and concluded that the specter must have carried off his bride. Two of the domestics corroborated the opinion, for they had heard the clattering of a horse's hoofs down the mountain about midnight, and had no doubt that it was the specter on his black charger, bearing her away to the tomb. All present were struck with the direful probability, for events of the kind are extremely common in Germany, as many well-authenticated histories bear witness.

What a lamentable situation was that of the poor baron! What a heart-rending dilemma for a fond father, and a member of the great family of Katzenellenbogen! His only daughter had either been reaped away to the grave, or he was to have some wood demon for a son-in-law, and, perchance, a troop of goblin grandchildren. As usual, he was completely bewildered, and all the castle in an uproar. The men were ordered to take horse and scour every road and path and glen of the Odenwald. The baron himself had just drawn on his jack boots, girded on his sword, and was about to mount his steed to sally forth on the doubtful quest when he was brought to a pause by a new apparition. A lady was seen approaching the castle, mounted on a palfrey, attended by a cavalier on horseback. She galloped up to the gate, sprang from her horse, and, falling at the baron's feet, embraced his knees. It was his lost daughter and her companion—the Specter Bridegroom! The baron was astounded. He looked at his daughter, then the specter, and almost doubted the evidence of his senses. The latter, too, was wonderfully improved in his appearance since his visit to the world of spirits. His dress was splendid, and set off a noble figure of manly symmetry. He was no longer pale and melancholy. His fine countenance was flushed with the glow of youth, and joy rioted in his large dark eye.

The mystery was soon cleared up. The cavalier (for, in truth, as you must have known all the while, he was no goblin) announced himself as Sir Herman Von Starkenfaust. He related his adventure with the young count. He told how he had hastened to the castle to deliver the unwelcome tidings, but that the eloquence of the baron had interrupted him in every attempt to tell his tale. How the sight of the bride had completely captivated him, and that to pass a few hours near her he had tacitly suffered the mistake to continue. How he had been sorely perplexed in what way to make a decent retreat, until the baron's goblin stories had suggested his eccentric exit. How, fearing the feudal hostility of the family, he had repeated his visits by stealth—had haunted the garden beneath the young lady's window—had wooed—had won—had borne away in triumph—and, in a word, had wedded the fair.

Under any other circumstances the baron would have been inflexible, for he was tenacious of paternal authority and devoutly obstinate in all family feuds; but he loved his daughter; he had lamented her as lost; he rejoiced to find her still alive; and, though her husband was of a hostile house, yet, thank Heaven, he was not a goblin. There was something, it must be acknowledged, that did not exactly accord with his notions of strict veracity, in the joke the knight had passed upon him of his being a dead man; but several old friends present, who had served in the wards, assured him that every strategem was excusable in love, and that the cavalier was entitled to especial privilege, having lately served as a trooper.

Matters, therefore, were happily arranged. The baron pardoned the young couple on the spot. The revels at the castle were resumed. The poor relations overwhelmed this new member of the family with loving kindness; he was so gallant, so generous—and so rich. The aunts, it is true, were somewhat scandalized that their system of strict seclusion and passive obedience should be so badly exemplified, but attributed it all to their negligence in not having the windows grated. One of them was particularly mortified at having her marvelous story marred, and that the only specter she had ever seen should turn out a counterfeit; but the niece seemed perfectly happy at having found him substantial flesh and blood—and so the story ends.